THREE TO PLAY

Kris Cook

MENAGE AMOUR

Siren Publishing, Inc.
www.SirenPublishing.com

A SIREN PUBLISHING BOOK
IMPRINT: Ménage Amour

THREE TO PLAY
Copyright © 2010 by Kris Cook

ISBN-10: 1-60601-760-8
ISBN-13: 978-1-60601-760-9

First Printing: April 2010

Cover design by Jinger Heaston
All cover art and logo copyright © 2010 by Siren Publishing, Inc.

ALL RIGHTS RESERVED: This literary work may not be reproduced or transmitted in any form or by any means, including electronic or photographic reproduction, in whole or in part, without express written permission.

All characters and events in this book are fictitious. Any resemblance to actual persons living or dead is strictly coincidental.

Printed in the U.S.A.

PUBLISHER
Siren Publishing, Inc.
www.SirenPublishing.com

DEDICATION

To my pre-reader, Angelina Hicks-Carter. Thanks for your insightful input.

To Jim Shafer, for the music you create.

To Mike Cintron, Michael Elderkin, and Al Blackwell, great friends who always listen.

To my mentors and friends, authors Melissa Schroeder and Shayla Black. Thanks for all your great advice on writing and the business…and for never hesitating to kick my butt.

And to Stephen, for always believing in me.

THREE TO PLAY

KRIS COOK
Copyright © 2010

Chapter One

Clint Moore walked into the radio station's control booth and smiled at the shiny, black and stainless steel equipment. Very cutting-edge for a market this size. Nice. Best of all, no Beth Taylor. At least not yet. Not that she mattered.

Due to his agreement with the station's management, he'd have to allow her a trial period on the show he usually shared exclusively with his pal, Dustin Lake. They made a successful broadcasting duo that stations brought in to boost sagging ratings. He had no plans to make it a trio. After a few weeks, he would demand Beth's dismissal from the morning time slot. Wouldn't be the first time.

"You must be one of the new guys." Said the overnight announcer, who looked to be in his mid-fifties, gray hair matching his mustache.

"Clint."

"You're early. You even beat Beth." The announcer extended his hand. "I'm Ted."

He shook Ted's hand. "Nice to meet you."

"And the other guy on your team?"

"I always come in earlier than Dustin. I like extra prep time for the show."

Clint looked at the digital clock on the wall. *Three-fifteen a.m.*

Their airtime started at six, but he always arrived early. Dustin, who buzzed in near show time, give or take thirty minutes, constantly laughed about that.

Though they saw things from opposite sides of the universe, they'd been close friends since college.

"Good luck today." Ted smiled and donned his headphones.

Most anyone would find the overnight guy easy to trust. Clint rarely let his guard down. Besides, he and Dustin would only be around long enough to learn names and boost ratings, not long enough to remember anyone once they'd gone to the next assignment.

The other man turned his mic hot. "You're listening to ninety-four point seven FM, Talk Radio. I'm Ted Scott. Today's forecast, cold, temperatures dipping to…"

As Ted gave the weather, Clint quietly moved to the adjacent studio, the location of most of the station's live broadcasts. Three positions for the announcers, with mics, keyboards with flat screens, and comfy chairs faced each other. Two other spots for guests rounded out the space. Clint spotted the chair he would claim: the one facing the control booth window.

"Don't even think about it." A female's voice jolted him from his inspection.

He turned and found one helluva sexy woman standing by the door, glaring at him. He guessed early thirties. Piercing blue eyes. Dark shoulder length hair half-tucked under a ball cap. Her lips were plump, naked, and naturally red. Nicely curved body. She wore hip-hugging jeans that clung in all the right places. A snug V-neck icy-blue sweater made her full breasts impossible to ignore. A wave of hot lust coursed down to his dick.

"About what?" he said as innocently as he could muster.

"That chair. It's mine." She arched a dark brow. "At least for the time being."

This was day one of the new gig. The pissing match had already begun.

"You must be Beth Taylor."

"In the flesh." She cocked her head to one side in defiance.

And boy, what flesh. How amazing it would be to plunge deep into her. Every move she made pulled at him. His dick responded in record speed as he imagined how she might look cuffed to his bed as he stuffed every one of his inches into tight pussy.

Clint frowned. He never mixed business with pleasure and never had difficulty restraining his hormones. Something about Beth jacked with his control.

Unacceptable. He needed to keep his mind on business.

"Which one are you?" Beth flung each word like a dart.

Already he liked her. No beating around the bush, just in-your-face brashness. He'd always had a thing for slightly older women, hot and comfortable in their own skin, like Beth.

"Clint Moore." He pointed to the closest chair to him. "This one will work for me."

"What are you, twenty-one?" she scoffed.

He sat, hoping Beth hadn't spotted his arousal. "I turned thirty a couple of weeks ago."

Beth rolled her eyes and walked around to *her* chair. Then she plugged in her headphones and waved at Ted behind the glass. "How old is the other half of your duo?"

"There's a month difference in age. We're old enough to be good at our jobs." He heard the steel in his voice and hoped she did too.

"Well, we should lay down some ground rules for you *boys*."

Boy? He'd love to lay her down and show her differently. And rules? Hell yes—but his, while she learned to call him master.

"We'll wait for Dustin."

Trying to have a conversation that made any sense when more heat pulsed into his dick would be next to impossible. The woman and her confidence were getting to him. Clearly used to calling her own shots, Clint itched to bend her to his will, to tame her. Visions of her tied up, spread-eagle and ready for him swamped brain.

He needed to find his bearings. Once Dustin arrived, he could let his friend charm Beth. That was his buddy's gift. Clint had other talents.

"You need backup to work this out? Hoping to double-team me?" Beth glared at him. "Don't think I'm a pushover."

Double-team? Clint and Dustin had been drunk a few times and shared women. They never stayed too long in any market to develop a relationship, so ménages happened. Expedient and fun, though the encounters leaned to a tamer side of sex than Clint typically enjoyed.

Above it all, he and Dustin had one rule: no sex with other announcers. Especially not this announcer, no matter how badly he suspected having her between him and Dustin naked and moaning would be amazing.

Damn. He shouldn't be thinking about fucking Beth. His job was to minimize her role on the show, not coax his way into her panties.

In the past ten years, only two other stations made them take on the current time slot holder. Every underperformer had been relegated to a less important time or canned altogether inside a month. Clint didn't care which fate befell Beth. He had a goal: land a job on New York radio, to ink a syndication deal, make it big. When it happened, only Dustin would be by his side.

* * * *

Clint Moore didn't just piss Beth off; he got under her skin.

He didn't look like any announcer she'd ever worked with. Short brown hair, matching goatee. Carmel-colored eyes. A square jaw. He wore a white button-down shirt that couldn't hide the killer body underneath. At least four inches over six feet, muscled chest, biceps as big as her thighs, a perfectly round butt that made her drool. He looked built for a football field, not a broadcasting studio.

Corporate had made it very clear that he and his friend would join her on the station's morning show. She wasn't dumb. She knew that meant she was fighting for her job. Worse, Clint, a man ten years her junior, affected her libido.

The hot stud adjusted the microphone's height so it lined up with his sexy mouth. No wonder he and his friend dominated the female demographic. Every in-person broadcast at a car dealership or new store opening would ensure the women stayed tuned in and turned on. No doubt Candi, the station's program director, would put that handsome face on billboards beside every major freeway in the city.

All last night, she'd strategized how this meeting would proceed. Boy, she'd missed the mark. She hadn't expected him to be so scrumptious. For him to throw her off balance.

She needed to back away, think and wrap her head around a new plan.

Why the hell did he avoid her interrogation? It seemed highly unlikely that she intimidated him. His demeanor of careful restraint told Beth that he rarely let anyone get to him and that he retained tight control of most situations. She must not allow him that power, or she'd be just another casualty of Clint Moore and Dustin Lake.

"Why are you afraid of some harmless questions?" Beth challenged.

"Beth, trust me. You want to wait. I'm not here to be your buddy, and I don't give a shit what you think. If you want a conversation, it will go better with Dustin. He's more..." Clint frowned, clearly in thought.

Was she tripping up the whiz kid? Goodie.

She pushed him. "What?"

"Affable."

She couldn't figure out his accent. His diction seemed to place him as a native of the Midwest, but some of his phrasing seemed like he might be from New England. She'd known many radio broadcasters who worked to change their accents, thinking it would help their careers. According to the boss, real or not, Clint absolutely delivered ratings that soared to the top of any market he invaded. She wasn't surprised that he sounded so damn sexy.

"If you can't handle it, I'll wait." Beth looked down at her notes, but she wouldn't wait for long. She didn't have much time. According to Google and her broadcasting buddies around the country, Moore and Lake left a trail of unemployed announcers in their dust. Beth refused to go down without a fight.

Taking in a breath, Beth planted her hands on the desk. She dared not pick them up lest Clint would see her hands shaking. Her reaction stemmed, in part, from anger. How dare he come into her studio and think he could run her out. The other part? Well, a woman couldn't help but appreciate such a fine specimen.

"Until Dustin shows, where can I get some coffee, Beth?"

God, his voice could hypnotize anyone, no matter how unwilling.

"Out that door, turn left. The break room is at the end of the hall." Was he testing her with the little request? Damn, she'd answered too quickly. Like she was *his* subordinate.

"Got it." He stood up and stretched his massive arms over his head, revealing the most delicious slice of his six-pack.

A wave of light-headedness swept over her. Clint took two steps to the door before Beth shook her head. She would *not* lose herself to some schoolgirl fantasy. Corporate may be in charge of the station, but Beth would not willingly turn the reins of *her* show over to this hotshot or his absent friend. Best he learned the pecking order right now.

"Bring me a cup, too." An order, not a request. She smiled tightly.

He raised a brow, as if acknowledging that he understood her game and found it amusing. "How would you like it?"

Naked. Sweaty. She cleared her throat. "Cream. No sugar."

He turned, and she lasered in on his butt. *Oh my God.*

She better get a grip. He was the enemy. His name now held top billing in the new morning show, not hers.

Beth couldn't imagine how much salary Candi gave the new duo, but it must've been enormous. Ratings ruled broadcasting, and paychecks. Always had. Beth eked out some good numbers over the years herself. In fact, until the arrival of the two men, she'd expected to continue delivering the best ratings at the station. But for the past two years, she'd slipped a few points. Nothing too alarming, but Beth felt the pressure, especially since the family who had owned the station for years sold out to an Atlanta-based national conglomerate six months ago. With Candi running things now...

When the door shut, she let out a long sigh just as Ted walked in.

"You okay?" The man had thirty-five years in broadcasting. He'd had his own share of moderate successes. But now, marrying late in life to a night-shift nurse made overnights ideal. Lucky for him, no danger existed of being squeezed out of a job. Beth wished she could say the same.

"Perfect," she answered. "How else would I be?"

He smiled. "I know this isn't easy. Just see where it takes you, Beth. You never know how it might work out. You might even learn something."

"From that football jock? I don't think so." She usually played life safe, but now, faced with losing her morning slot to Clint and his buddy, they forced her to act.

Ted shrugged.

She must execute her plan to be assertive with precision. Given Clint's forcefulness, she should ponder crossing the bitch line. Beth couldn't lose her morning slot or her job. Where would she find a new one that paid half as well? Given the current economy, stations simply continued to cut back.

The door from the hallway opened. She expected to see Clint returning with their coffees. Instead a different man walked in. Auburn, wavy hair, clean-shaven, vivid green eyes, six foot two. Muscles bulged from a brown t-shirt sporting a Corvette with the words *Vette Lover*. His cargo shorts hung low, revealing a bit of sun-kissed skin between the bottom of the tee and the top of the shorts. Instead of a briefcase, he carried a backpack. He looked like he had been engineered for a life lived to the fullest.

"*Darlin,* you must be Beth," the man said in an unabashed Southern drawl.

He smiled wide and spread his arms apart, inviting her for a hug like a long-lost friend. For some insane reason, she imagined walking into them and burying her head against that hard chest. If she did, would he comfort her? Kiss her? Ravage her with his amazing body? She shook her head to clear her mind. The wayward thoughts must stop. He was enemy number two.

Chapter Two

Beth Taylor, Dustin thought. *Damn. More like, Beth smoking-hot Taylor.* "Or have I wandered into the wrong station?"

What curves! How he would love to spend long hours exploring each and every one.

The older guy next to Beth smiled openly. "She's the woman you're looking for, and this is the right station. I'm Ted. Overnights."

Beth tilted her head to one side. "And you must be the name in the show's number two position, Mr. Lake."

She said it with venom. But he could sense something else. Was she intrigued? Excited, perhaps?

"Ouch." He put his hand to his chest. "Please, call me Dustin. *Mr. Lake* is my father."

She looked down, but he spotted the smile tugging at the corners of her lips. That pleased him.

"Beth, I didn't pick the show's title. I don't give one damn where my name goes. All I want is to have fun."

"Fun?" She sent him an incredulous stare.

"Yeah." Dustin had some very wicked ideas about the sort of fun he'd like to have with her, and they had nothing to do with the show. "You can't take this stuff too seriously."

She folded her arms over her chest, her blue eyes belying her irritation. "You blow it off, then. All I care about is getting good ratings."

Just like Clint.

Dustin sat his backpack down on the table. "If you live by the ratings, you'll die by the ratings."

"I'm gonna like you." The older guy offered his hand.

Dustin took it and smiled in return.

Beth glared at the overnight guy.

"Pleased to meet you, Ted. Look forward to working with you."

"Same here, Dustin. Good luck to all three of you today."

"Thanks."

Ted left, and Dustin turned back to Beth. Strong-willed and fiery, and exactly the sort he loved in bed. Heat flooded down to his cock as the door behind him opened.

"Dustin, you're here nearly two hours before show time?" Clint walked in balancing two cups of coffee.

"Yep." He smiled proudly.

Their byplay seemed to raise Beth's temperature. "Now that everyone is here, time to cover my ground rules."

Dustin fought to control his lust. He found confidence in a woman so damn sexy. "Ground rules?"

Clint sent him a tight smile. "Beth feels we need to outline how the three of us are going to operate."

"Okay with me." Dustin liked her sassiness. Liked her kissable lips. Thick. Full. Moist.

She turned to him. "Good. First, this is my chair. I've already informed your sidekick. Are we clear?"

Dustin nodded, half-listening. He could only imagine what heat lived under all her iciness. If he could thaw her out, what warmth and softness would he find? God, he'd love to devour those unbelievable lips, dine on her amazing breasts, and pull moans of delight from her throat as he filled her pussy with his cock.

"Dustin, are you listening?" Beth's voice blasted.

He nodded, lying.

"Second, I want prep time together. At minimum, an hour."

"Two hours would be better." Dustin wanted as much time with her as possible.

Clint turned to him. "*Two* hours? You hate prep."

"With you. But with her, I could learn to love it." Dustin sent her a wicked smile.

Beth raised a brow. "Two hours it is. Every day. Finally, I will have veto power about what goes on the show."

Clint stood up. "Not happening. If anyone is in charge in this studio, it's me."

Dustin put up his hand. Most likely, Clint would get Beth moved to another time slot by month's end. Until then, best to make sure their close proximity worked to his advantage. If he didn't defuse their ticking bombs fast, things could really go bad with these two. If he succeeded in getting them to change their tone, he might even get some fringe benefits from his new co-worker. *To hell with Clint's rules about not sleeping with other announcers.*

"Hold on, buddy. I think having veto power is a good thing, but not just for Beth, for all of us." Dustin winked at Beth.

Her eyebrows shot up.

"You do?" Clint drawled, looking less than pleased.

"Yep." Dustin couldn't hold back his wicked grin. "My first veto is for those jeans of yours, Beth."

Her face showed confusion. "What?"

"Your jeans. I don't want you wearing them. In fact, I think you shouldn't cover any part of your sexy body. I veto all of your clothes."

Clint's jaw tightened. Anyone else might have mistaken it for anger. Dustin knew better. Beth was exactly the kind of woman Clint went for.

Beth rolled her eyes. "Can we please stick to topic, and not your Penthouse fantasy?"

"Darlin, don't you think it's best to make up the rules as we go?"

Beth glared at him. "I thought you two were professionals. Perhaps I was wrong?"

"We are," Clint barked.

Dustin liked how she got to Clint. Even better, he could tell that she unsettled him. The thought of seeing his friend lose all that restraint was its own form of excitement in Dustin's mind.

"You don't seem terribly professional to me. I know what kind of ratings you've delivered in the past, but that doesn't mean you can duplicate those here." Beth turned back to Dustin. "I know what it takes to succeed in this city. For the past ten years, I've held the number-one talk radio time slot in the market. Putting together some house rules is a way to start off on the right foot."

"Then you know, Beth, that making great radio is more about chemistry than some list of self-imposed regulations." Dustin loved her passion. If he could translate it to the mic, they'd be smoking. Even better if they could translate it to the bedroom.

Clint sipped his coffee, looking calm. Based on his buddy's tight grip on the cup, Dustin didn't buy it for a second.

Finally, Clint unleashed the daggers. "A number-one time slot is impressive. But the management brought us here for some reason. Maybe settling for number one isn't enough anymore."

Beth tried not to wince at Clint's comment, but she failed. Dustin could almost see the wheels turning in her head. She'd try another tactic to gain control. This woman would not cave quickly. He liked her all the more for it.

She took a pencil and tapped it on the desk. "Let's start with the most important request I have for *our* new show, Dustin."

"I'm listening to every word from your delicious mouth."

Beth sighed, then pursed her delectable lips. "I've heard that you're the flirt of the two."

So she'd studied up on him. He smiled seductively. "Guilty."

His dick hardened just imagining her naked and under him.

She raised a dark brow. "Just so you know, with me, not happening."

"Aw, now where's the fun in that?" he mocked.

"I'd ask you to shut up, but I doubt you will."

"He won't." Clint ratted him out.

"At least keep your *hot talk* off-the-air. It won't earn us ratings."

Dustin disagreed. He'd love more verbal foreplay with the gorgeous Beth. In fact, that sparked an idea. Yes, Clint had been the brains in their past jobs, but Dustin possessed the instinct to know what worked for the audience. His gut told him that the three of them would blow the ratings lid to the roof if he ignored Beth's request and gave the audience a heavy dose of scintillating *tête-à-tête*.

Dustin sent her a bright smile. "Hot talk is exactly what we'll be doing, darlin. Get ready."

* * * *

"Beth, so you're admitting you would enjoy some two on one action in the bedroom?" Clint cocked his eyebrow.

"I said that I would *consider* pushing various boundaries should the right opportunity present itself. I didn't specifically say anything about two on one." Her cheeks heated at the thought.

"But you didn't say you wouldn't, either. What you need to convince you are two guys who have experience in that arena." Clint's stare paralyzed her. "What do you say?"

"You expect me to believe that you and Dustin have been there, don't that. Right."

"At your service," Dustin announced.

She scoffed, but her belly pulsed. Were they serious? God, Clint and Dustin in the same bed? With her? A hot shiver ran through her. She'd never given menage much thought. But they certainly made her think about it now—hard and heavy.

"In your dreams," she said. "Besides, you couldn't handle me."

"If you're challenging me, you know how I'm going to respond." Clint's tone unsettled her. "You don't have the faintest clue what we could handle. But I guess you're saying you'd be too afraid to try."

"That isn't what I said at all." Beth fought off the frustration that grew with each passing minute. "You're twisting my words. Again."

"Then tell us what you mean—*exactly*." Dustin sent her a wicked stare.

"So you can willfully misunderstand me again?" She'd lost the battle about setting down ground rules, but she'd be damned before she waved a white flag. "I'd rather not."

"So you're a tease. I knew it."

"I'm not a tease. Look at the clock."

"Beth, I'll always take time to *push boundaries* with you."

She felt her cheeks heat up, partly from anger. The other part, she didn't want to think about. His unabashed lust for her pulled at her own desires. And Clint didn't affect her any less. How long had it been since she'd been with a man? Eight months, and only one time before that since the divorce five years ago.

"Dustin, we'll have to pick this up tomorrow," Clint interrupted.

Tomorrow? How many tomorrows on the morning show did she have left with these two? Why was she letting hormones get to her when her job was on the line?

"Hmm. I just know Beth's got a lot more to share with us."

The way Dustin looked at her made her heart stutter. Her lust thickened, and she tried to fend it off. No luck.

Clint's shuttered expression hid his heat…almost. Damn, with both of them in the room talking and exuding sex, she couldn't think straight.

"I know she does, but we are out of time today. I'm Clint."

"I'm Dustin."

"And I'm Beth."

Clint concluded, "Thanks for tuning in to ninety-four point seven FM, Talk Radio. We'll be back tomorrow morning at six."

Warm tingles slid down her spine with every word from Mr. Tall-Dark-and-Dangerous.

"Have a great day," Beth added.

Dustin winked at her. "And a wicked night."

Her stomach flipped somersaults. God, the cowboy got to her.

They both did, but in different ways. *I'm acting like a fool.*

The red light went dark. Instantly, the speakers blared the teaser for the midday show. The engineer in the control room killed the sound, and gave a thumbs up to all of them.

Dustin nodded back at the guy.

She stood up. "You're an asshole, Mr. Lake."

"I am?"

Was he trying to sound innocent? If so, he failed. In the past few hours since meeting him, she'd gotten a glimpse of how sinful he could be. If he ever turned the full force of his charm on her, how the hell could she resist?

She needed to control her anger and lust, or the first day with these pricks on *her* morning show would be her last. She swallowed her irritation and paused. What next? She must persuade them to accept her as a part of the team.

"Of course, you're an asshole, but aren't most men?" She turned to Clint. "At least the phone lines lit up like a Christmas tree."

His eyes darkened. "That usually happens when we show up."

"Not on the very first day. The audience loved it. The three of us burned up the airwaves." Dustin laughed.

Clint didn't respond, but fixed his hard stare on her. A cold chill spread through her. From nearly boiling to an ice cube in seconds. Not good. She needed to act fast.

Dustin she could win over, but how could she convince Clint to keep her on the show? Perhaps if she got Dustin on her side? After all, if he wanted her on the air with them, how could Clint refuse?

In the past three hours she'd learned their unique dynamic. Dustin's talent on-air amazed her, like a live wire of energy and flirtatiousness contrasted with Clint's controlled sensuality. Clint never faltered, hinting at something hidden and formidable underneath all his discipline. She understood why they'd been so successful. The juxtaposition of their diverse personalities produced something that magnetized any who listened. Being near them, she felt totally wowed—but also terrified. The morning had been intense and unnerving. She missed her safe routine, knowing what would come next.

Work your plan, Beth. Revise as necessary. Don't get sidetracked.

"I enjoyed our first day together," she lied.

Dustin stretched his arms above his head. "I've not had this much fun on a show in a very long time."

Clint glared at her. Did Dustin's statement piss him off? *Damn it.* If he perceived she was trying to put a wedge between them, she'd be off the show before she got a chance to win either of them over. She needed to tread lightly.

"Still, can we move the topic to something besides sex tomorrow?"

"Nope," Dustin said flatly. "This worked today and it will work tomorrow. I think we might have something pretty amazing. Let's keep exploring that and see where this takes us."

Beth crossed her arms over her chest. Her wishes weren't swaying them, so maybe logic would. "I don't want to get on the FCC's bad side."

"Just keep it to innuendos, and we'll be just fine. Besides, I haven't heard of anyone being seriously fined since Stern."

Beth didn't like it, but he was right. The hotter the talk, the more the phones lit up. Maybe playing along *was* her best strategy.

Bright expectation flooded into her like warm Caribbean waters. If listeners loved the chemistry, Clint and Dustin might let her stay on mornings. Not that she wanted to be known for sexual banter, but times were desperate. *Could it be that easy?* Once they finished a couple of rating periods, they'd be off to their next job. If she could survive until then, maybe she'd get her show back. And she needed that. Her job made sense, the only thing in her life that did.

Then she spotted Clint throwing the morning notes into the trashcan, apparently angry. "Dustin, let's not veer from what works for us."

Us? The way he emphasized the word made it clear he meant he and Dustin—minus her. He slammed the lid on her hope.

"You're the one who always says we need to keep the show fresh. Well, today topped every single one I've been a part of."

Clint folded his arms across his chest. "Let the ratings tell us what is fresh and what works."

So Dustin liked the idea of keeping her around. Beth wanted to smile, but didn't. Perhaps later, he'd even break ranks. She needed to exit and let them continue their argument.

"Guys, I'll see you two tomorrow."

"Wait. How about grabbing a bite to eat with us?" Dustin made a gesture of spooning food into his mouth. *So playful and sexy.*

Clint cocked an eyebrow. "We have a meeting with Candi, Dustin."

"Fuck that. I'm starving."

"Fine. I'll take care of it. Do whatever you want."

"Beth, you and me. Food. Sound good?"

Trying to stay on the show felt like walking a tightrope. If she made a single misstep, she'd fall to the ground and lose everything. Refusing Dustin now, when he might be her only ally, didn't seem wise.

"Okay."

"Clint, you sure you won't go with us?" Dustin asked.

No answer. Instead, he turned and left.

Chapter Three

Candi leaned back in her chair. "Clint, I'll work on it, but there's an issue with Beth's contract that the lawyers need to work out."

Clint didn't give a damn about lawyers or contracts. "Just get it done."

"But the three of you sounded fantastic this morning. The calls even went into overflow. That has only happened when we gave a car away a couple of months ago."

"Don't you think that's a result of the advertising campaign you launched before we came?" He wanted to believe that, but suspected otherwise. The show had been electric. He clenched his jaw.

"Maybe, but I think this combination works. It's just your first day here. Try it for a few more days."

Beth was proving a more worthy opponent than most. Instead of caving whenever he and Dustin threw her curve balls on the air, she knocked them out of the park. The more time Clint spent with Beth, the more he wanted her wet for his taking. The thought radiated heat to his cock. *Fuck*. He hated this lack of control. He wouldn't allow it.

Obviously, she got to Dustin, too. If Dustin broke their rules, things would get complicated and fucked up—fast.

She must to go to another time slot.

"I don't care how you do it, just make it happen. I'll give you a week."

"It'll take a month."

"Candi, I know you can get this done faster."

She pursed her painted lips in a mulish expression. "I need a month."

Clint wasn't backing down. "Two weeks."

"Impossible."

"I have no doubt you can work miracles."

She sighed. "I'll try."

"If you can't make it happen, then per our contract, we walk."

"Dustin wants her off the show, too?"

His buddy had no idea that Clint had acted already to cut Beth loose. The way Dustin tripped over his tongue whenever Beth was around, Clint didn't want his buddy to ever know.

"I manage our careers. Dustin is okay with that, so repeating this conversation to him won't do a bit of good. Nor will telling Beth. If you do, we'll walk. The station will have no morning show with Moore and Lake."

Candi glared at him. Maybe he'd pushed too hard, but he had to. He couldn't spend another month with Beth. Hell, a week was pushing it.

"She's a good employee and a popular announcer. I have no grounds to fire her."

"I don't want her fired, just moved to another time slot." Not ideal since she'd still be around the station. Still, she'd be easier to avoid if she were on another show.

"Okay, Clint. I'll figure something out with the attorneys. I hope you know what you're doing."

He did: saving his duo with Dustin and his own sanity.

*****

Dustin listened to Clint deliver his closing line. "Thanks for tuning in to ninety-four point seven FM, Talk Radio. We'll be back Monday."

"Have a great day," Beth added.

As Dustin had done since the very first show, he winked at her. "And a wicked night."

Every one of his attempts to seduce Beth off-air fell like a ton of bricks.

The red light went off and the speakers quieted.

He turned to his co-announcers. "Can you believe we've only been on air together for two weeks?"

Neither Clint nor Beth answered. His buddy glared. She shuffled papers, refusing to look at him.

Damn.

Their time together burned up the airways. They knew it. He wanted to add Beth permanently to the mix professionally—and personally. But as the show's ratings rocketed through the stratosphere, Clint's mood grew more sullen. Beth had admitted to Dustin that, regardless of results, she didn't believe management would keep her on the show much longer. Dustin would have to work harder at convincing Clint to expand their duo to a trio. Otherwise, Clint would do his dirty work and Beth would be gone.

He smiled broadly, hoping it might be contagious. "It's like we've been working together for years. We sound great, and I'm having a blast."

But the tension he felt between Clint and Beth told him they weren't. No matter what he tried, he couldn't get them to lighten up. Only when the mics went hot did they show any spark. And then fireworks boomed.

He needed to think of something, or one of them would soon explode on air and slaughter their chemistry.

Dustin looked up just as Candi walked into the studio from the hallway.

Attractive? On the outside, maybe. But on the inside? He knew the type. Candi's career ruled everything. Not that ambition was a bad thing, but clearly she wasn't climbing the ladder through mere hard work and talent. He imagined that the woman would walk over the bodies of dead friends, though he doubted she had any, to get what she wanted.

She sat in the guest chair closest to the door. "Though it's early, corporate decided to run a phone survey last night. If the numbers are anywhere close to correct, in the next rating cycle you guys will dominate this time slot in all the key demographics in the entire market. We might even get a five to ten point gain with the twenty to thirty-five year olds."

"In just two weeks?" Beth's jaw dropped.

"Yes," the boss lady answered. "Congratulations, guys."

Beth looked up with a smile, but he didn't miss the flash of disappointment in her eyes. "I guess you were right about the innuendos, Dustin. Congratulations, boys."

He turned to Clint. His friend's face showed satisfaction and something else. *Regret?*

That look worried Dustin. What the hell had Clint done?

Then he turned back to Beth. "And congratulations to you. You're as much a part of the success as Clint and I."

He meant it. Though he and Clint had always made great radio together, Beth being in the mix produced something that far exceeded anything they'd ever fashioned before. She kept them both hopping with her stinging questions, quick wit, and sexy voice. With her, they'd created not just something good, but spectacular.

Now, Dustin craved something beyond the professional from Beth. An image of her naked and waiting on his bed had been flashing neon in his mind for the past two weeks. After several glances at Clint, Dustin knew his friend shared the same desire. A night with Clint and Beth would be unparalleled. And might be just what they needed to cut the rising tension and get his co-announcers talking to each other.

"Thanks, Candi. We're thrilled, of course," Clint added, but his tone belied something else. Something hidden. What?

Dread sliced at Dustin. The entire two weeks whenever the microphones went live, Clint's delivery blazed, sharp, masterful, always directed at Beth as if he couldn't wait to get her naked and begging. The second the broadcast stopped, Clint's demeanor dropped to twenty below zero. Yes, he leaned to the serious side, but he'd hit an icy chill since arriving at the station. And today his cold shoulder had grown even worse. The North Pole would be balmy next to him.

"You're welcome," Candi answered. "And since we have two birthdays to celebrate today, I thought I'd take all of you to lunch."

"Two?" Beth asked.

Candi stood up. "Yes, yours and Dustin's."

He and Beth shared a birthday? He'd never given his birthday much of a thought, but now Dustin couldn't help but smile at the idea it gave him.

Maybe he could use their shared birthday to spur Beth and Clint to better moods. Beth wouldn't dare deny him his birthday celebration—and hers. All the three of them needed some time away from the station to really get to know each other, one step in bringing Clint and Beth together.

He decided to go for it. "Happy birthday, Beth. I've got an idea."

"Happy birthday to you, too. But your ideas scare me." Beth unplugged her headphones. "Thanks, but no thanks."

"We have to celebrate," Dustin informed. "This is a decade birthday for me. Goodbye twenties."

"Big deal. It's a decade birthday for me, too. I'm leaving the decade you're entering and the last thing I want to do is celebrate," Beth said, then turned back to Candi. "I appreciate the offer, but I'm beat. I just want to go home, have a bath, and put this day behind me. I hate birthdays."

He just couldn't let Beth not commemorate the day. She needed her spirits lifted, and he would gladly accommodate.

"I love birthdays. It means you're still alive." He turned to Clint for agreement. "Right, buddy?"

Clint glared, saying nothing.

"Beth, you might as well give in." Dustin insisted. "I won't let you off the hook."

Just then, Candi's cell rang and she stepped out in the hall. "Important meeting, gang. Sorry. Another time."

When the door closed, Dustin commented. "She is always so…"

"Corporate." Beth offered, brow arched.

"Exactly," Dustin agreed.

Clint glared at them both. "Candi is the boss. And she hired us, Dustin. Or did you forget?"

"That doesn't mean she's someone I'd like to socialize with, especially after she half-heartedly offered to take us all to lunch to celebrate for Beth's and my joint birthday. I bet she thought of some hamburger dive to fill the bill. Candi should be taking us to dinner to some swanky restaurant for lobster or steaks. Hell, and for drinks, dancing. We're on top of the ratings, which makes her look good, and it's our double decade birthday."

"Do you always get your way?" Beth sounded exasperated, but he saw her smile lurking.

Dustin smiled back. He'd never tire of that sight. She seemed almost relaxed. Definitely sexy.

A fresh wave of craving moved through his cock. "Today, at least. Besides, forty or not, you're one hot woman."

She smiled. "You're such a liar, Dustin Lake."

He must push for more. For victory. For conquest.

"Forget Candi," Dustin said. "The three of us are going out on the town. Don't even try to say *no*. Your words tell me that you don't have any plans. And a decade birthday is a big deal. We'll have a blast, I promise."

Beth rolled her eyes then turned to Clint. "Does he have an off button?"

"No. I've known him since college. The good thing is Dustin never breaks a promise. So, as he put it, you should have a blast." Clint scribbled something on a piece of paper and handed it to Beth.

"What's this?" she asked.

"My cell number," Clint answered. "I'd give you Dustin's, but since he always forgets to charge his, mine is a better choice. Text your address. I'll put it in the GPS for him."

"For him?" Beth frowned. "Unless you join us, I won't go. You know what a player he is."

Clint's eyes darkened. "Not a good idea."

"What do you think will happen if he comes over alone?" Beth put her hands on her hips.

Oh, he'd have her naked and satisfied in an hour.

By the way Clint gritted his teeth, he knew it. "Fine. I'll come, too."

Dustin couldn't help but smile. "Good. It's settled. We'll pick you up at seven."

A night out together would do the trick. These two *would* fall in line with his ultimate want. Dustin couldn't wait for the dessert.

"Okay." Beth raised her arms to the ceiling with her hands clasped.

Her breasts rose, and heat rolled through Dustin. Then Beth let out a long yawn. Even that seemed sexy. His dick hardened.

"We're going to have an incredible time," he vowed.

Beth hands fell to her sides. "It's got to be an early night. I'm beat."

"I agree." Clint cast Dustin a glance, as if willing him to silence.

Not likely, buddy.

Beth continued, "But I don't want steak. I want Chinese. And I don't want to go out. I want to watch a movie. Something funny."

Dinner at her place? Even better. Dustin grinned. "Great idea."

He'd make sure that Clint's sour mood and Beth's birthday blues would get swept away tonight. They needed a good dose of fun. It might take some coaxing on Dustin's part to sweeten these two grouches. Birthday cake and sex ought to do the trick.

The best birthday present for him would be unwrapping Beth out of her clothes. Dustin let his imagination run as he pictured her naked and willing between him and Clint.

That would be the best birthday present ever.

Chapter Four

Standing outside Beth's apartment building, Clint glared at him. "Dustin, it's not going to happen."

Clint had been arguing with him all day. And he refused to believe it.

"Why not?"

"Not with Beth. You know the rules."

"Your rules, not mine."

"What do you think will happen if, by some miracle, she lets us take her to bed tonight?"

"Amazing sex."

"Maybe, but if she doesn't agree to it, then what?"

Argue all you want, buddy. "She'll agree. I'm good at persuasion."

"And what about after? It's going to be awkward. Even if we fuck her, I won't concede to keeping her on the show. Period. If that's what you're hoping for, drop it now."

"With the numbers we're getting, I don't believe Candi will remove her from mornings. Let's sideline that topic for later."

Dustin wanted Beth and had no doubt that Clint did, too, regardless of his protests.

Sharing women wasn't new to them, but Beth wasn't like any woman he'd ever known, with or without Clint. Dustin believed Clint would grab the opportunity to fuck her, should it arise. And if he didn't, well, a night alone with Beth would be an incredible runner-up.

Dustin took the single flight of stairs up to Beth's door. "Let's just see where the night takes us."

Clint stepped behind him and grabbed his arm. "Dammit, you aren't listening. I know you want her. But I am not going there. Got it?"

"Settle down. I'll take the reins tonight. You just sit back and relax."

Before Clint could respond, Dustin broke free and knocked on Beth's door.

Every day at the station, Beth wore a baseball cap with her hair in a ponytail. But when the door opened, her long, dark locks hung loosely to her shoulders and her eyes sparkled. His hunger multiplied, refusing to be curbed.

Dustin looked over at Clint. His friend's eyes were locked on Beth like handcuffs.

Deny all you want, pal. You want her as much as I do.

He turned back to Beth and winked. "We're going to make this the best birthday of your life."

* * * *

Beth half expected to start drooling over Clint and Dustin standing outside her door. They held some DVDs, two bottles of wine, Chinese takeout, and a birthday cake. Clint wore a dark blue, long-sleeved dress shirt with black pants, and for the first time since she'd met him, Dustin wore something besides shorts. Instead, he'd donned jeans that clung to the right places and a knit, short-sleeved collared shirt.

Delicious duo, indeed.

Something warm and mushy filled her chest when she spotted the words on the rectangular dessert underneath the plastic protector. *Happy decade birthday, Beth.*

Fortified with the news that Candi shared that morning about the phone survey, Beth demanded Clint come with Dustin tonight in hopes of sealing her place on the show. Dustin hinted that he wanted to keep her on mornings. With Clint, she had to meet him on a logical level. With the survey information that women, ages twenty-five to forty-five, liked her on the show, Beth could now make a strong case to him. Without her, Clint and Dustin would deliver good ratings. With her, they'd be fantastic.

If after tonight Clint still didn't want her with them, she hoped Dustin would side with her. The more she thought about it, discord between these two might be the only way. She didn't like this tactic, but couldn't think of any other way to remain on the show she loved.

Beth felt like her mind was spinning on a carnival ride. She'd insisted on staying in rather than going out. Home field advantage. Also, she'd thought she'd be able to keep a lower profile in her own home than in one of the city's nightspots. Now, she worried about her self-control. If she gave into the desires that Dustin kept fanning, would Clint think she was trying to sleep her way to a permanent place on the show?

"May we come in?" Clint asked.

Being a consummate broadcaster of fifteen years, she kept the nervousness out of her delivery. "Yes, of course."

This wasn't how Beth wanted to spend her birthday, being reminded of the impossible. Forty years old and having wicked thoughts about the two men, ten years her juniors, who were taking over her morning time slot and sweet-talking her out of a job.

She stepped aside and motioned them in. "Set the food and the wine on the kitchen counter by the sink. You can put the DVDs on the coffee table."

Dustin smiled and walked into her kitchen as instructed. She couldn't stare at his incredible backside enough to satisfy her. Walking back into the living area empty-handed, he flipped his jacket over one of the chairs.

She turned to Clint. Her heart picked up pace at his powerful stare. Her knees weakened. Had he seen her staring at the cowboy's ass? Was he angry? He looked aroused. God, she could only imagine what a night with Clint would be like. Intense.

Being attracted to Dustin, while stupid, made sense. His contagiously happy demeanor entranced her, despite her best efforts to resist. However, Clint's taciturn bearing, even with his sexy, muscled body, shouldn't have any appeal for her. Yet she could not deny the potent pull he had over her. He'd drop any woman to her knees. The image of him bending her to his will shouldn't have any appeal for her. She swallowed. It did.

Dustin smiled. "Beth, your place is great. It's got your mark all over it." He pointed to the large painting over the sofa. "Very much you."

Her stomach flip-flopped. The canvas swirled with rainbow colors. Beth was proud of the piece, though she'd never told anyone that she'd actually painted it. Other paintings by legitimate artists decorated her walls. He'd chosen the only work of hers she'd ever hung. How had he picked up on how much it meant to her?

She hoped like hell she wasn't blushing. "I like it, too."

Clint still wore his black overcoat. His expression resembled a hunter's catching the scent of his prey. She swallowed.

"You staying, *pardner*?" Dustin asked Clint.

Clint hesitated, glanced at Beth, then nodded at Dustin as he slipped off his trench. "Do you have a coat closet, Beth?"

"No. I can hang it in my bedroom closet."

Beth held out her hand. He folded the garment precisely and handed it over to her. His scent permeated the fabric. Shivers ran over her skin.

"Thank you." His voice came out deep and rich.

He made her whole body buzz, as did Dustin. And now they were here, in her home. Tingles spread up her spine. How would she ever manage to keep this cozy night professional yet friendly when all she wanted so much more?

"You're very welcome."

"Where's your bottle opener?" Dustin asked.

"I thought I put it on the table before you got here."

"I don't see it, darlin.'"

That Southern accent drove her wild. Her brain short-circuited as heat spread into her pussy.

She wanted to smile at him, but didn't dare. Who knew where he'd run with that? His teasing and flirting had grown during their two week acquaintance, intensifying her wicked thoughts.

Every moment with Dustin and Clint exercised her self-restraint. Her gut tightened every time they got near her. On one hand, she should've remained pissed at these two gatecrashers. On the other, she could've quit, leaving the two to fend for themselves. But she hadn't done either. She wasn't sure why. Instead, she'd worked with them, desired them, staring at them like a golden pocket watch swaying on a chain, back and forth, until completely hypnotized. Having them in her house, all alone, with wine and Chinese food now seemed like a very bad idea.

She pointed to the other side of the table. "It was right there, Dustin."

"I see it there, on the floor." Dustin pointed. "I must've knocked it off with my jacket. Sorry."

He bent over to pick it up. A tingle spread up her spine as she enjoyed an even better vantage of Dustin's perfect butt. Damn, she needed to get it together.

Flushing, she turned away. "Don't worry about it, Dustin. Let me hang Clint's coat up. I'll be right back."

"And I will have wine waiting for you, birthday girl."

"Please stop the *birthday girl* bit. I really am not thrilled about today."

"Dustin, cut it," Clint ordered, then nodded toward her.

They both knew Dustin wouldn't, but she loved that he'd tried. It was the nicest thing he'd done for her since getting her that first cup of coffee. Since then his mood had turned more and more gloomy. He'd barely spoken to her, except when the microphones came on.

Then he turned a blazing sexual heat on her. Why, she couldn't imagine. Worse, she'd been unable to get either of them off her mind.

Beth walked into the bedroom and shut the door. She needed a minute. Several, actually. At that moment, slipping out her window didn't seem terribly crazy.

They were so different from Beth. She loved her routine, took comfort in it. Once the guys left for their next gig, she'd get her show back, if she wasn't shown the door first.

Hopefully, all she had to do was wait them out. The plan for tonight consisted of drinking a glass of wine, eating some Chinese food, watching a funny movie, and pretending to be pals. Once they were relaxed, she would make her case.

But her libido and active imagination seemed set on taking over. Internal fires scorched her when they looked at her like she could be dinner and dessert all in one. She needed to get her head back in the game.

Dustin had flirted with her from day one, on air and off. Which didn't necessarily mean anything. Flirting was like breathing to him.

Clint, though quiet, had locked eyes with her several times over the past two weeks. His tense stare always seemed filled with something hot. Anger? Desire? Or was it all her imagination?

On air, his force dominated. He guided the conversation masterfully, just like she suspected he did everything else. When Dustin moved out of bounds, he'd pull his friend in. When she balked or grew too quiet, he'd engage her. Though he held the reins of the show, off air he acted very differently. Like Jekyll and Hyde. Aloof, seemingly struggling with something. What?

She chewed her bottom lip.

Even more puzzling, on the show, Clint and Dustin had alluded to participating in three-ways. More than once. At first she thought they said it for shock value and ratings, but now, she wondered. Had they actually shared a woman together? Had they thought about sharing her?

It was foolish to wonder such things about Clint and Dustin. Professionally, she had too much at stake to even ponder the suggestion, much less act on it. Emotionally, even more. If they approached her, seduced her, would she have the will to refuse them? Or would it be like throwing gasoline on the growing bonfire building inside her?

Her heart pounded in her chest.

Determined to put the thought out of her head, Beth ripped open her closet, and took out an empty hanger. Instead of hanging the garment up, she pulled the fabric up to her nose and took in Clint's essence lingering on the coat. Spice and oak. The back of her neck tingled. Her rational side vacationed at least three states away.

"Birthday Beth, your wine is ready." Dustin's voice floated in from the other side of the door.

She placed Clint's garment on the hanger, hooked it on the rod, then she closed the closet door.

Decade birthday or not, Dustin had come with some feeble attempt to cheer her up. Did Clint only come along to keep Dustin out of trouble? Or did he have another agenda?

Chapter Five

The wine relaxed Beth and Dustin, though they'd only opened one bottle. Clint tasted some of the pinot noir, but more than half of the drink still sat in his very first glass. He couldn't risk imbibing more of the burgundy liquid. That would be much too risky with Beth sitting between him and Dustin, looking like something out of his midnight fantasies, blue eyes sparkling, breasts moving with each laugh.

While Clint held his outside motionless, his insides rolled like the tides. He wanted Beth, wanted her to experience pleasure the way he knew how to deliver it, controlled, with her bent to his will.

He suspected that she would respond to his handling, but that could never be, not with Dustin present. Clint knew better than to reveal his trips to BDSM clubs. Dustin, with his Southern upbringing, had specific ideas on how a man treated a woman. Cuffing and lashing weren't among them. Dustin would flip out if he knew exactly what Clint liked.

The comedy film Dustin had brought kept the birthday duo in hysterics. Clint had lost interest in the movie less than ten minutes into it. A talking dog didn't do a thing for him.

Still, he enjoyed hearing Beth laugh and watching her chest rise and fall under the green silk with each outburst. He imagined pinching her nipples until she begged him to stop. Whenever she drew even a fraction closer, his dick hardened.

He'd witnessed her quick wit, stinging candor, and unfaltering loyalty to the other announcers at the station. Though she'd kept her guard up since the first day, tonight, he sensed her practiced calm, unsettling him even more. Something was going on in her head…

Beth clearly enthralled Dustin. Knowing how badly his friend wanted her, Clint's lust accelerated. He wanted her naked, sandwiched between them, tied up, body writhing, and pussy wet.

Never going to happen.

His job was to do whatever it took to elevate him and Dustin to the top of the ratings. Being in broadcasting, one couldn't afford self-reproach or guilt. People got hurt. That was just a fact. Unfortunately, Beth's slot on the show threatened his and Dustin's success. Beth wasn't his concern. He owed her nothing.

At the next obvious joke in the movie when the dog came in contact with his nemesis, the singing cat, Beth leaned in closer to his side.

Dammit.

An overwhelming ache to plant a ravaging kiss on her lush mouth pounded inside him. Dustin shot him a glance, indicating similar thoughts ran through his head. No matter Clint's intention not to fuck her, Dustin refused to be deterred.

Clint didn't move, though lust grew inside him with each press of Beth's curvy body against his side.

She went against all his professional rules. More importantly, he deeply suspected that sex with her would be much more than a one-night stand. What *much more* might mean, Clint wasn't sure, but he could almost see the solid brick wall that loomed ahead, ready to come down on him like a ton.

Dustin turned Beth to face him. When he pulled her in closer, she stopped laughing.

Beth glanced over her shoulder at him, her blue eyes questioning,. Their gazes met, sizzling, before she looked again to Dustin.

In for a penny, in for a pound. Clint clenched his jaw even tighter.

"I'm tired of the movie, aren't you?" Lust filled Dustin's voice.

Clint considered ending the conversation before Beth answered. It maddened him, but curiosity killed his better sense. He remained silent—and waited.

Seconds turned to nearly a full minute.

As much as he desired her, Clint hoped her pause meant the evening would come to an appropriate close. That would be for the best. Maybe if he kept repeating it, he would believe it.

"Then I'd like to talk about my role on the show."

"Later." Dustin would not be thwarted from his desire. So very like him.

Beth didn't move from between Clint and Dustin.

Clint's heart pounded hard and fast. The collision seemed unavoidable. He needed to prevent it, but he couldn't find his voice. That was a lie. No, he didn't want to. Everything inside him ached to touch Beth.

Dustin moved closer. "I've got something better in mind."

Clint closed his eyes, looking for strength to push aside his mental images of them fucking long enough to stop this train wreck. "We should call it a night."

"I am tired." Beth whispered.

"Time to go." Clint glared at him over Beth's shoulder.

Dustin refused to take the hint. "Darlin, you're a very sexy woman."

She arched a dark brow. "I've heard that line before."

"Not a line." Dustin leaned into her, his face rapt. For once, he wasn't smiling.

Beth pulled away from Dustin, pressing her back into Clint's chest. Clint couldn't resist. He wrapped his arms around her, drawing her in closer.

Her body would felt soft and inviting, and her scent wafted over him. He breathed in her aroma, a light blend of delicate citruses balanced with fresh aquatic notes. He wanted to devour her.

"I think you're damn sexy, too." Clint's willpower faltered.

"No more empty compliments, please." Beth pulled away and turned to face Clint. "You guys are trying to make my birthday special. You already have. Thank you."

He'd treated her like shit for two weeks, and she'd mistaken that to mean he didn't find her attractive. The truth? She was much more than merely appealing to him. She was completely irresistible.

"You want to know what I really think?" Clint touched her cheek. "You're fucking unbelievably sexy. It's not bullshit, and it's not because of your birthday."

"Clint—"

Rather than let her finish her reply, Clint devoured her quivering lips. When she moved to free herself from the kiss, he pulled her in tight, crushing her lips beneath his. Their kiss would end when he decided, not her.

With a feminine gasp, Beth's eyes closed and her lips parted. He swept inside her mouth, tasting her nectar. She whimpered softly. His cock hardened.

Finally, he released her. "Beth, don't doubt what I say again. If I say you're sexy, you are sexy. Understand?"

"O-Okay," she breathed. "Guys, you are both very sweet to…"

Dustin leaned in and dove into her mouth. Beth released a muffled moan. Watching his friend put his all into kissing Beth stoked more heat in Clint. He wanted to dominate Beth. Completely. But damn if it wouldn't agitate Dustin. He'd have to back off and let his friend call the shots.

When Dustin stopped kissing Beth, he said, "You're the one who's sweet."

Clint visualized Beth pleading for him and Dustin to fuck her. The thought gouged at his self-control. His lusty mind told him to take another taste of her wet lips now. Monday, he'd fix everything with the boss because sex changed nothing. Beth couldn't stay on mornings with him and Dustin.

* * * *

Beth's head reeled. But before she could get her bearings, Dustin took another turn at her lips, lingering, teasing. Deepening, then pulling back. Pressing in harder, then softening. He awakened more desire inside her. Her pussy warmed and moistened.

When Dustin finally released her mouth, he looked over at Clint as if sending some invisible message to him.

Beth glanced at Clint standing mere inches away. He exuded carnality. Clint's stare compelled her to obey. Then he looked down to her breasts.

Her nipples pushed against the inside of her lacy bra, and though she didn't look down, she didn't doubt they were visible to Clint and Dustin, fully erect like an invitation, screaming out to be touched and tasted. But instead of moving in to accept, Clint's gaze returned to hers.

She'd always thought herself adept in reading body language, but with Clint, that skill failed her completely.

Beth felt like she floated in unfamiliar waters without a lifejacket. Kissing these two hunks had left her guard entirely down. They were the interlopers that threatened her safe, familiar world. If Candi found out about Dustin and Clint's joint mack on Beth, there would be major hell to pay.

All Beth needed to do to get her show back from corporate's dynamo duo was to stay cool, play the game, and not screw up. Beth only needed to outlast Clint and Dustin, and not give Candi any reason to pull her off mornings.

But what if they were orchestrating tonight as a way of getting her off the show sooner? No. Dustin wasn't capable of that deceit. Clint, however, was capable of anything.

"Are you guys hoping to get some more ammo tonight to embarrass me on air like you did this morning? Offering to be my guide. You were just teasing me."

Clint pinned her in place with a single stare. "I meant every word this morning."

For God's sake, she had ten years on both of them. Wisdom

should give her an advantage. But her years didn't equate to knowledge in this realm. Clint and Dustin *had* shared women before. Her stomach capsized. Things were moving at a breakneck pace. She needed to slow things down to a more comfortable, safe speed.

"I think we should have some cake."

"I'd rather nibble on your delicious neck," Dustin's hand drifted down her shoulder brushing the side of her breast.

Her breathing turned shallow as Dustin kissed her throat and caressed his way down to her inner thigh. If she'd chosen to wear shorts, as previously planned, instead of changing into pants, Dustin would be touching her skin, mere inches from her mound. The thought caused her ache to grow.

"Dustin, please." The words slipped out of her mouth. She bit her lip. Too late to call them back.

"Yes, birthday girl?" Dustin tormented, his hand inching closer to the juncture of her thighs.

"I am not sure we should do this."

"What should we do instead?" Dustin teased. "Maybe this?"

His left hand moved to caress her shoulder, cup her neck in his warm palm, while his right hand roved higher up on her thigh. Beth's pulse quickened. "You like that?"

"Yes, but…"

"Or do you like it more when I touch you like this?" His hand left her nape and tunneled under her shirt, caressing her stomach. Goose bumps popped up everywhere he touched her.

"I do, b-but…"

Dustin leaned into her ear. "What about this? Do you like this?"

He caressed her lace-clad breasts and began nibbling on her earlobe. His breath skated along her neck. Sparks danced over her body.

"Y-yes. But we need to…"

"And this?" Dustin pulled her blouse away to reveal part of her shoulder and then kissed every inch of exposed skin while cupping her breast.

She wanted to answer him, but all she could muster was a nod. Her body fired, lit by Dustin's words, caresses, and kisses.

"You're amazing, Beth. I want every part of you. From your lips, to your breasts, to your navel, to your tight, hot cunt," Dustin whispered lustily. "I'm dying."

I'm dying, too, but this is craziness.

And what about Clint? After they kissed, he hadn't said a word. What was he thinking?

When Beth looked over her shoulder at him, his eyes filled with desire, but he didn't move to answer that want. Did he think she and Dustin were going too far? Her body tensed.

Dustin turned to Clint. "Don't you think Beth is amazing, *pardner*?"

"She's..." Clint's voice trailed off. "Yes."

Beth watched his eyes darken with some internal conflict that gave her pause. "Guys, we should stop. This is something I've never done before."

She imagined a wicked night with Clint and Dustin would be amazing and adventurous, but once over, the two men would soon be off to their next job, their next conquest. Office flings never ended well, but they always ended.

Clint stared at her with rich brown eyes. He knelt down and cupped her shoulder. "Is that what you really want, Beth?"

God no! "It might be best."

His voice turned stern, commanding. "That's not an answer. What do you want?"

Dustin continued to caress her stomach. With each gentle circle, his hand got closer and closer to... "Please. Tell us, Beth."

She could hardly take a breath for the excitement zipping through her. The kissing had melted her like butter. And now, these sexy men demanded an answer.

What *did* she really want? For things to go back to the safe, the familiar? Turn back the clock a month earlier, before they'd arrived?

Yes and no. She did want them. But at what cost? This would lead nowhere. Self-doubt crept inside her and took a seat.

Dustin kissed her neck, jolting her from her thoughts. "Don't be afraid."

"I'm not." Beth lied.

"Beth," Dustin cajoled. "It's all right. Clint and I will give you everything you need."

"I'm nervous."

Clint sat down next to her, kissed her neck, then whispered in her ear, "A little nervousness will add to your pleasure."

Her gut turned several somersaults.

"Beth, you have nothing to fear with us." Dustin leaned in and kissed her again. First, like an exuberant guest, then like an owner. Heavenly. Amazing. No one had ever kissed her like that before.

With Clint's lips nipping at her neck while Dustin continued to penetrate her mouth, she shivered with delight. She most certainly would've slipped off the sofa if they hadn't held her.

Dustin paused, his green eyes boring into her. "Clint and I are going to push you to beg for more."

"Bragging, are we?"

"Promising." Clint's voice rang like steel. "We'll explore your pussy and gorgeous ass, every part of you, with our tongues until you're soaked with desire. We'll leave you totally spent and satisfied."

Shivers rolled throughout her body. If she did agree to one night of complete abandon with these two, was she risking her future at the station? A gamble she shouldn't take, but her mind felt like a fast-spinning whirlpool.

"Oh, yes, we are," Dustin's voice filled with a new lustiness that only added to her growing ache.

"You'll be screaming before we're done." Clint grabbed her wrists and held them above her head.

"Screaming isn't really like me." Tremors traveled through her body.

"That's gonna change. And when you think we're done, and you can't take any more, we are going to fill you up again, completely." Dustin's voice lowered with growing lust.

"He's right. We'll leave no part of you untouched." Clint's hand moved from her arm, to her shoulder, and then to the top button of her blouse.

The dam broke inside her. How the hell could she say no to that?

Tingles wrapped around her body like a net. She looked down at her chest as Clint unbuttoned her blouse, one button at a time. Slow. Easy. Her nipples hardened under her bra. A frenzy grew inside her.

Beth watched both men's breathing tighten. Her body quaked with anticipation. This could get out of hand very quickly. She needed to grab what little control remained in her.

"But if I do ask you to stop?" Beth bit her lip.

"You won't," Clint shot back.

"But if I do?"

"We'll stop," Dustin assured her.

"But you won't ask. I'll make sure of it," Clint growled. Holding her wrists, he guided her hands to his chest. "Touch me."

Her heartbeat sped up. "Y-Yes."

Clint's eyes were filled with pure lust and power. He was in testosterone overdrive and her feminine side loved it.

When her blouse fell open, exposing her bra and bare belly, Dustin's fingertips brushed her underwire and Clint's mouth caressed the top swells before he pushed the cup aside and latched onto her nipple, pinching it between his teeth. Wetness seeped from her pussy, and a throbbing rumbled inside her.

Watching Clint's every move, Dustin moved his hand up and cupped her other breast. She held her breath, melting when he pressed his thumb on her nipple, moving in tight circles. Beth tilted her head back. Heat ran up and down her body. Want chained her resistance and gagged her doubt. God, they were amazing.

A shameless ache burned behind her soaked panties. If she didn't stop this soon, she wouldn't be able to.

Chapter Six

Every passing second, Clint's lust for Beth grew, reaching epic proportions. Clearly, Beth was wrangling with her own desires, an act of futility. Like trying to hold back millions of gallons of water from the top of Niagara Falls from plunging into the giant pool below, this wasn't something either of them could stop.

"No more *buts.*" He gazed at Beth with her shirt agape. "Close your eyes, Beth."

She obeyed his order and her blue eyes disappeared. Her lashes seemed to dance from excitement.

"This is going to be the best birthday ever." Dustin exclaimed.

Clint vowed to himself to deliver on that promise. He unbuttoned her blouse and stripped it off of her.

At the sight of her torso completely exposed, his heart thundered, his dick lengthened, and his breathing deepened. Beth's perfect skin looked silky, soft. Layering his mouth over hers, he reached around and unlatched her bra.

Clint felt a sudden surge of heat, as he and Dustin each slid a strap off Beth's shoulders, exposing her naked, supple breasts. Her nipples burned a rosy red. Now, not only did her hands shake, but so did her entire body.

"Darlin, you're perfect," Dustin growled.

"Nervous or excited?" Clint's cock throbbed.

"A bit of both." She folded her arms over her breasts.

Clint took her hands and made her uncross her arms. Then he turned to Dustin. "You like what you see?"

"Fuck, yes. Look at her. So beautiful."

Beth remained silent, her eyes shut.

"Open your eyes," Clint commanded her.

Her deep blues opened and first looked at Dustin. Then she turned to him. The need to touch every inch of her body taste her juices, lick her clit until she exploded, left him dizzy.

Clint traced Beth's lips with his finger. Voluntarily, she puckered up. He leaned in and replaced his finger with his own lips. Though the kissing before aroused him, their current mouth-play made him sizzle and burn in a way he never had. His cock hardened as she sucked the tip of his tongue. He tightened with desire like a string on a bow near breaking.

Continuing the kiss, he moved his hands over her chest. Finding her nipples, he took the bits of flesh between his fingers and thumbs and pinched lightly. Her swallowed her mouthwatering moan, dying for more. Powerful urges moved through him, unfettered, demanding release.

He broke their kiss, and dove down onto her left breast. He licked the erect nipple and then sucked on it hard.

"My God!" she exclaimed.

He moved back up, covering Beth's mouth with his own, taking her breath into his chest. Moving his hand to cup the breast his tongue had just tasted, Clint felt his self-control fraying.

When he released Beth's lips, she sent him a sexy smile.

"You two are quite the duo." She laughed. "How can a woman refuse?"

"Yes." Dustin's voice sounded full of want, deep as a well. "We're going to do this.

He stood up, ripped off his shirt and tossed it away. Beth reached up and touched his chiseled stomach. His stare revealed a craving Clint had never seen in him before. Beth also seemed juiced up to a feverish pitch.

"Hmm."

"We're going to cover you in kisses, darlin. We're going to taste every inch of you. We're going to fill you up completely until you've come for us so many times you can't remember your own name."

Clint had never seen Dustin so on fire before. Very dangerous. He had to keep his head. He wanted her, but his lust could not be left unchecked. Tonight's sex must be a first and last. No more.

Clint stood up. He stripped off his shirt, folded it, then placed it by the couch.

Turning back to the action on the couch, he watched Dustin cover Beth's nipple. Her body quivered. They looked amazing together, his olive skin and an arousing contrast to the pale ivory silk of her flesh.

He'd let Dustin take the lead. Clint needed to sit back and cool a bit. Instead, his own fire just kept growing and growing.

* * * *

Beth couldn't believe that she actually sat in her apartment bare-chested with Clint and Dustin, also naked from the waist up. Her mouth ached for more kissing, her nipples for more suckling, her pussy for what was coming.

She continued her exploration with her fingers of the guys' hard-muscled chests. A night with these studs would free her to experience total wantonness.

Really?

She'd never let herself go completely, not with any man. And with two? Before tonight, she would've doubted it could ever happen. But here she was, half-naked on her sofa, not with just one man, but two. She couldn't help but grin at the twist fate served up.

Clint knelt in front of her. He rubbed her thighs, then moved his hands to the top button on her jeans.

Oh God.

Her panties were soaked. Was she ready, mentally, emotionally, for such intimacy with Clint and Dustin? True, they were the hottest guys she'd ever seen. True, they were in her apartment, ready to pleasure her. True, it had been long months since she'd had sex. But...

"Wait." Beth grabbed Clint's hand.

He stilled. "Exactly what am I waiting for?"

"Just wait a second." Her voiced sounded weak as doubt rolled through her.

The floor seemed to be shaking, but that wasn't what shook. It was her body.

"Shall I count to ten and then ring a bell before I dive down between your legs?" Dustin teased and sent her a wicked smile.

Beth's lips quivered. Not from fear, but from passion. Why did she always stop everything whenever it ventured into the unknown? And this went way beyond anything she'd experienced. Somehow, she knew they'd take her to a place where she not only orgasmed, but utterly surrendered. Still, her judicious side wouldn't be quieted.

"This may not be a good idea."

"You're right." Dustin smiled and then licked his lips.

"I am?" A mix of relief and regret zoomed through Beth. She crossed her arms over her bare chest.

"It's not a good idea." Dustin leaned into her.

"Right." Her stomach jumped up into her throat, as if she rode an elevator in free-fall.

"It's not a good idea." Dustin put his lips against her ears. "It's a *fan-fucking-tastic* idea."

Beth's smile widened as her imaginary elevator started back up to the penthouse level.

"Time to get this party into full swing." Dustin shucked his jeans faster than a lightning strike.

White briefs could not hide his monster erection. Beth felt her eyes nearly pop from her head.

Desire filled Beth from top to bottom. She wanted them. Hungered. Why was she holding herself back?

"We need some protection." Beth squeezed her legs together.

Dustin and Clint both smiled broadly. Dustin grabbed his jeans and reached into the front pocket. He pulled out four condoms. "This will be a start. How many do you have, Clint?"

This will be a start?

They'd actually come expecting she might fuck them. Instead of being angry, excitement shot through her like a bullet.

"Enough." Clint pointed at Dustin. "Since this guy has set the pace, it's time for me to take off the rest of my clothes."

"O-Okay." It took all her willpower not to jump up and rip them off of him.

"Then I am going to take off *your* remaining clothes."

Her appetite multiplied with every tantalizing second.

Clint peeled his pants off and tossed them to the floor. Boxers. The head of his cock stood out of the waistband.

All that control she'd seen the past few weeks masked what loomed inside him. Instinct and heat. Intensity.

If she didn't hold herself together, he'd overwhelm her in minutes.

Clint unbuttoned her pants and slid them off. His fingers skimmed along her thighs. Goosbumps and a hot zing followed his hands. When her pants cleared her ankles and puddle on the hardwood floor, her arousal clamped tight inside her.

Dustin slid next to her on the couch, kissing her shoulder.

Beth looked down. She'd chosen pink panties. Her cheeks heated to a temperature of an iron on the hottest setting. On the front of the delicate silk, her desire left a large damp spot. Before she could cover it, Clint dove over the material with his mouth. Every cell in her body began to roar, to electrify. His tongue on the fabric lashed her clit underneath. She cried out.

"How does that feel, darlin?" Dustin murmured, kissing his way up her neck.

"A-Amazing. More. Please…"

Dustin stroked her hair. The guy could be so gentle, so kind. And yet so dangerous.

"Tell me what you're feeling, Beth." Dustin said, as he moved his hands to her nipples and latched on.

"Light-headed," she panted. "Excited."

With his dark eyes full of promise and raw desire, Clint ripped her panties away. An instant later, Dustin darted between her thighs and laved his tongue over her clit. Her mouth went lax, insides doing somersaults. Gripping the soft silk of his hair in her hands, she moaned.

"Do you want more?" Clint's mouth on her breast erotic torture.

Dustin drove her wild with his tongue on her clit.

She wanted to answer, but with both men tonguing her to new heights of intoxication, she couldn't.

She couldn't hold back another second. A vibration swirled inside her. "Y-Yes!"

Clint and Dustin didn't ease up on her. Their mouths worked magic on her, and her orgasm exploded from her core to every nerve ending.

After a bit, her climax faded back. Her breathing steadied.

"You came for us. Good." A hint of a smile showed on Clint's face. "Just the first of many."

Every whisper seemed to wander over her skin, raising goose pimples along the way. And the way he caressed her, kissed her, spoke to her blew her mind. A total tease at the outset, but he'd delivered, even as he reassured her.

Clint kept her on edge. He was more urgent, focused, as he took her mouth again. He never seemed to tire of her favorite activity. She closed her eyes as he deepened his kiss. When she opened them again, she saw his dark eyes staring back, unblinking, intense. He'd take and demand, then exact more. At that moment, she doubted herself. Could she satisfy such a man? Beth's body stiffened at the thought.

As if sensing her fear, Clint gently slid his hand up her thigh while continuing their kiss. As his fingers skated over her mound, settling in firm circles on her clit, she tensed again, this time neither from fear or unease. Instead, the infinite want these two men extracted from her made her rigid all over.

Clint continued his friction on her clit. Another climax took her.

"G-God!" Tears fell from her eyes. Detonations from the orgasm erupted inside her.

"That's it, Beth." Clint whispered. "Let yourself go. Feel everything. There's more to come. Much more."

When her climax quieted, Beth locked gazes with Clint. She imagined him hungry, ready to pounce.

He lifted her up from the sofa as if she was made of air. She could feel his rock-solid arms, one around her shoulders, the other beneath her knees. She leaned her head into his chest.

"Time to move this to the bedroom." Clint's voice, low and measured, seduced.

Dustin nodded. "I agree."

Beth's toes curled. The bedroom. She knew what would happen. Here, in her living room, she might still be able to stop them from moving horizontal. But in there?

Still, she couldn't find the will to end the evening. Instead, she leaned her head into Clint's muscled shoulder. He carried her into the bedroom. Dustin tossed her bedspread and blankets to the floor. Only the sheets remained, waiting for their naked bodies to intertwine.

Clint placed her on the bed. The two men gazed down at her naked body, their cocks granite-hard. An urgent need sizzled throughout her body, like a forest fire out-of-control.

"She is so fucking hot." Dustin dove next to her. His dick pressed against her side.

"That she is." Clint joined them on the bed, sandwiching Beth between them.

Four hands wandered over every part of her, touched, owned. The pleasure ripped through her like a lightning bolt of heat, searing her to the core. They gave her more than anything she'd ever experienced before, and the enormity of it scared her. Still, her pussy ached, readying for Clint and Dustin.

The thought of the duo filling her up and being completely connected to them made Beth tremble. She wanted them, and they wanted her. She sped past the warning signs in her mind that read *Danger* with red flashing lights.

Clint touched her shoulder. "You want to taste me, Beth."

Chapter Seven

Beth leaned down and consumed the head of Clint's cock.

"Yes. That feels so good." He wanted her like no other woman before, wanted her in ways he'd never known possible.

She clouded his mind, his reason, his purpose. But the clouds she brought also contained the promise of sweet release.

The selfish bastard he knew himself to be melted next to Beth. In fact, his will weakened just being near her. Now, with her naked body next to his, skin to skin, all his resolve to stay removed simply vanished.

Beth's mouth left his cock, and she pumped him with her hand. His forthcoming orgasm grew linking him to her. Something about this moment with Beth and Dustin pushed him past his old limits. He closed his eyes and focused on her fingers squeezing his dick. But he couldn't let his guard down completely.

"Slow down, Beth. I don't want to come right now." Clint turned to Dustin. "You should experience her mouth, too."

"Would you like that, Dustin?" Beth's hand remained on Clint's cock.

"Oh, yeah. More than you can imagine."

Clint watched Beth blanket Dustin's cock with her lips. As she continued pumping Clint, her head bobbed on Dustin's dick.

Oceans of urges swirled through Clint. Unlike anything he'd ever experienced before, this was more *connected*, almost like he could feel Beth's anxious arousal and Dustin's skyrocketing need. He'd never been this attuned to his partners. That scared the hell out of him, but his clawing lust shoved reluctance to the curb.

He stroked Beth's soft hair, kissing her shoulder as she worked Dustin over with her mouth. Heat boiled from Clint's gut as he watched Beth shower Dustin with pleasure, tempting him to throw caution to the wind.

Stay on course. Don't veer.

Dustin grabbed two handfuls of Beth's hair and fucked deeper into her mouth.

Clint knelt behind Beth. He began kissing her back and rubbing her round buttocks, sliding his fingers to the wet, waiting flesh of her pussy beneath. More desire rolled through him.

"Beth, I want to taste your sweetness," he whispered to her.

With her between him and Dustin, Clint saw her skin flush red. His body echoed her heat.

Clint guided Beth back to a pillow. Moisture coated her slit. He couldn't wait another second.

The second he got his tongue on her, Clint moaned. She tasted sweet. With a lusty gasp, she gripped his shoulders, nails digging into his skin. She wanted more, and he resolved to give it to her. The sound of Dustin sucking on her breasts only added to his rush.

He grabbed Beth's hips and pulled her closer, going deeper with his tongue, fingers sliding in a slow tease over her clit.

He pressed on her clit.

"O-Oh, y-yes." She licked her lips.

"That's it, Clint. Make her moan."

Clint wanted to please Dustin and Beth, and also wanted more for him. His insides boiled.

"I've got to get inside you, Beth."

"God, yes," she said in a breathy rush.

He climbed over her, his dick in hand. He spread Beth's legs farther apart and guided his pulsing cock between her slick folds, up and deep inside her. Her cunt tightened around his dick like a vise.

"Clint, you feel so good."

He focused on the frenzy inside him. He went slowly into Beth's tight cunt. How he wished he could make this moment last forever.

He watched every expression on her face. Each provided clues to what she wanted, and was ready to take. Whenever she bit her lip, he knew he could give her another inch of his dick. When he finally was able to fill her up with his dick, he watched her lick her lips. Everything about her drove him wild.

Clint rolled to his back, pulling Beth with him, his dick still in her pussy.

"Beth, I want to watch you blow Dustin." He shove up into Beth again. She sat up and took every bit, whimpering with need.

"Will you stay inside me while I suck him?" Her eyes sparkled.

In answer, Clint leaned in and devoured her left breast, then whispered across her skin, "Trust me. I'm not going anywhere for a long while."

"G-God." Beth's body shook as she continued riding Clint.

"Get closer, Dustin, to make it easier for her."

Dustin came into Clint's peripheral view.

Beth turned her head and swallowed Dustin's cock. A wave of energy passed through Clint. The sexy display breathlessly burned him deep down, they were bent on stoking the fire. *Burn, baby, burn.* His psyche spiraled faster and faster and his climax loomed.

Clint's lust boiled up inside him as he continued sliding in and out of Beth's pussy.

Dustin moaned and fisted the dark comforter. For an instant, his and Dustin's eyes locked. Suddenly, fear rose inside Clint. But before it could shackle him, luckily, Dustin turned back to Beth and raised her enough to kiss her.

A rush moved through Clint as he watched the two deepen their kiss.

When their mouth embrace broke, Beth grabbed Dustin's thighs and looked at them both with wide, dilated eyes. Beth's pussy tightened around his dick.

"I-I'm g-going to…" Beth panted.

"Me, too," Dustin growled, sliding back inside her mouth.

"Come!" Clint commanded.

The dam broke inside him, and he came as the other did, with curses, writhing bodies and hoarse shouts.

After a few minutes, the pulse of his orgasm slowly eased and his muscles relaxed.

"That was amazing." Dustin reached out and touched his shoulder.

Something akin to electricity fired through Clint from Dustin's fingers on his shoulder.

Fuck.

Clint jerked his entire body away from Dustin. Too late. The memory that he'd buried years ago surfaced and froze every cell inside him. He stopped breathing. His tongue turned to sandpaper.

"Everything okay?" Beth panted.

She must've sensed the change, too.

Clint pulled his spent dick out of Beth's pussy and rolled onto his side.

"Everything is just fine," Dustin answered. "Right, pardner?"

"Fine." Clint pushed the new sensation and the old memory far away.

"I'm glad." Beth smiled at him.

"It's my birthday, too." Dustin grinned wide. "I want some more, please."

Clint's breathed deeply, relief rolling over him.

"Beth, you want to give this cowboy *more?*" Clint asked to cover up the moment.

"Well, we *do* still have more condoms." She grinned.

Dustin dove between Beth's legs and lightly teased her clit with his fingers.

"Easy, cowboy."

Clint breathing relaxed, relief rolling over him as the moment passed without Dustin and Beth wondering more about why he'd reacted to his buddy's brush against his skin.

Just don't touch me again, Dustin.

* * * *

Beth still buzzed from the uninhibited sex she'd enjoyed with Clint and Dustin. The afterglow took her to a dreamy state that she resisted leaving.

Where Clint had been demanding, Dustin had been adventurous. They'd shared her, been inside her. The night had been off-the-charts. Though they were different in their lovemaking styles, each reached her in ways she'd never felt before, and she wanted to explore that more.

Dustin's body pressed against the full length of her back, arm wrapped around her waist. Though his slow breathing let her know he still slept, his hand seemed awake, gently massaging her breast, causing her body to charge up again.

Beth heard the door to her bathroom shut. Her gut tightened, evaporating her remaining dreaminess.

She opened her eyes. No Clint. A minute later, she heard the shower start.

Her heart pounded hard and fast. Had she made a mistake? Would they think she'd taken them to bed only to protect her job?

Shit. Wasn't the proverbial morning after a bitch?

That wasn't the reason. But why did she agree to have sex with them? Though multiple opportunities for bed partners had come to her since her divorce three years ago, she'd only had sex twice since then. Had she been so pent up that when Clint and Dustin offered to fuck her, she jumped at the chance?

She'd wanted them from the very first day, no matter that they would likely push her off the show. Something about their masculinity and self-assuredness called to her. Dustin's innuendos heated her to a boil. And Clint? Something lived underneath all that willpower, something commanding she could respond to. But he hadn't unleashed it yet. Why, she wasn't sure, but his sudden rush to the shower just confused her more.

Beth tried to peel Dustin's arm around her waist off without waking him. His breathing changed.

"Are you trying to get away?" Dustin growled and nipped at her neck.

Her ache came back with fervor.

"No. Should we wait for Clint?"

"Why? He's the one who left." His lips touched her ear, and he whispered, "Plus, he takes very long showers."

His hands drifted to her nipples. He tweaked them lightly with his fingers.

"Beth, we'll have time with him again. Right now, I've got a hard dick that won't be denied your tight pussy."

"Hmm."

Dustin slid his hand down to her mound.

"And by the feel of it, you're ready for some hot action from me, too."

She had no idea how, after such great sex hours ago, she could want more, but she did. "Mmm…"

He positioned her back against the mattress and placed his legs on either side of her hips. He leaned down and pierced her mouth with his tongue, which worked her like a hot, sumptuous tool. She felt his hard cock touch her folds. Her body shuddered, her ache growing.

He broke their kiss. "You're so fucking incredible, Beth."

"If you mean how I kiss, I'm not bad, but neither are you." Her heart pounded rapidly, engulfed with desire.

Dustin cemented their lips together again. No one had ever kissed her like this, so playful yet captivating. His savory kiss went on and on. When he finally lifted his head, his gaze clung to her like ivy. Her desire grew again, unfurling like petals on the first day of spring.

Beth caressed his naked chest, fingers scratching lightly over his skin.

"Darlin, I want to be inside your hot pussy."

Beth smiled. Dustin held no boundaries or secrets. Sharing whatever entered his head came natural for him, which was so unlike her.

"This time, slow and easy." Dustin moved and guided the tip of his dick to her swollen folds.

"I'd like that." Beth touched his shoulder that felt like solid rock.

His cock eased inside her. She tightened her inner wall around his massive erection.

"Y-Yes, Beth. I feel you. So good."

He filled her up, especially now that she was a bit swollen and tender after last night. Dustin began a slow, methodical grind, but she wondered if he could hold out for long. God knew she couldn't.

Soon, his body glistened with a fine layer of lusty sweat. Passion tightened his face, blazed his eyes, as it rose up inside him. She shivered expectantly.

"You like it slow, Beth?"

"Yeeesss," she moaned.

"You're like the sweetest sugar," he panted pumping slowly in and out of her pussy. "Can you handle this pace a bit longer?"

Handle it? Beth loved it. She nodded.

He clenched his jaw, his fists. His effort to make their connection last pleased her.

Beth's heart pounded wildly as passionate intensity inside her increased from his steady glide. In and out. In and out. So incredibly deep. She bit her lip, relishing his vigorous, unchanging rhythm. His entire body rocked against hers with each charge. Amazing willpower.

Never changing or ceasing his drive, Dustin leaned down and pressed his lips gently to hers. Their tongues danced. Want exploded inside her like a grenade and her body thirsted for him.

"You're ready, I can tell. Come for me, Beth." Against her chest, his heart pounded into overdrive.

"Do it, Dustin. Fill me up."

Her whole body rocked, inside and out. The bed squeaked. The mattress shook. Beth thought the bed might break from his handling, but she didn't care. She wanted him, wanted this.

Every muscle in her body tensed as desire spiked deep inside her. The pressure grew, built, expanded, and she mewled with need. "Come for me, darlin."

Beth held her breath as the climax spread through her. Fresh tears spilled from her eyes as she cried out with a dazzling fervor.

She watched Dustin's body tense, his eyes close, then she felt him thrust into her pussy as his orgasm exploded. He moaned in her ear, still pushing inside her. Then, seconds later, his body shuddered, slackened. Beth caressed his back.

Tonight more than made up for her recent drought in the bedroom. A three-way and a two-way in the same night. Amazing.

Suddenly, she realized that no sound came from the bathroom. She glanced toward the bathroom. Clint stood in front of the open bathroom door. His dark eyes blazed fury.

Chapter Eight

Clint turned off the water, and the sounds of lovemaking pierced his ears.

He decided that before he opened the door, he should turn off the light to let his eyes adjust to the dark. When he twisted the handle and swung the door open to the dimly-lit bedroom, he found Dustin fucking Beth.

At the sight, enormous desire exploded inside Clint. His cock hardened and his flesh heated. When the water first hit his skin in the shower, he wondered if he'd made a mistake by giving into his lust. Watching the last few seconds of Dustin and Beth fucking on the bed gave proof of his total blunder.

The past two weeks left no doubt at the type of handling Beth needed. He believed she enjoyed her control in the world, but though she might not know it, yet, would love to be controlled in the bedroom.

Images flooded into his mind of paddling her ass until the flesh turned bright pink, of tweaking her nipples hard, of fastening her to the bed with straps, of slapping her mound, of delivering pleasure in the way that would undoubtedly elicit delicious responses. Though he'd trained several women in the past, breaking down Beth's resistance would be more wicked, more amazing.

That could never be. Dustin could never see that side of him. Never. That remained his personal secret, among others, though Beth's moans and Dustin's growls tempted him to join them.

More hot lust marched down to his dick, but he took a breath, pulling in his icy-cold anger. It steadied him and his head cleared.

Had Beth feigned sleep until he left the room in order to have another go with Dustin alone? A kind of divide and conquer tactic to save her job? Probably. Beth was smart. Clint couldn't deny how perfect that strategy would be.

He watched as Dustin's body went rigid and Beth followed with her own orgasm.

Clint's body went taut, but no longer from desire.

Beth turned to him, looking surprised at his presence. She flipped the switch on her bedside lamp and wiggled out from under Dustin.

After Beth freed herself from Dustin, he spotted Clint and sat up. "That's the fastest time in the bathroom I've ever known you to take."

"Are you coming back to bed, Clint?" She brought her knees up to her chin, feet planted on the bed, arms circled around her legs.

With one hand Dustin silently motioned Clint to move closer, and with the other he gently stroked Beth's hair.

"Everything okay?" She tilted her head and leaned into Dustin.

Clint hated how sexy she looked, hated the power she possessed over him, hated that they looked so perfect together. *Too perfect.*

It wasn't too late to get back on track for his plan. One night with Beth couldn't destroy all his hard work. He'd get Dustin away and talk about their career strategy. Convincing Dustin would work, like always. They needed to pursue their dreams of success, and that wasn't Beth Taylor.

He caught her stare, fixed on him like a vise. *Fuck.*

"I'm leaving." Everything inside him hit the rocks when it came to her. He must get away, far away.

His plan for him and Dustin teetered on the brink. If she wanted to create a wedge between them, it might be working. Dustin's continuous touching of Beth's leg indicated he wanted more, and what if *more* meant a traditional coupling, not a three-way?

"You're not pissed that Dustin and I..." Her face showed an uneasiness he'd never seen from her before.

"Do whatever you want." He consciously controlled his voice. "I really don't give a damn."

But he did. He wanted her, like the condemned wanted amnesty, and that scared the hell out of him.

"Come on, Clint. Tell her that you're not pissed." Dustin swung his feet to the floor, exposing his half-hard cock. His face showed confusion. "We're all having fun, and I'd like to have some more. Wouldn't you?"

"It's late. If you want to stay, then stay. I need to get back to *our* place."

Before Dustin could speak, Beth pulled the sheet over her. "Go with him. I'm tired, too."

"But I'm not ready to go yet." Dustin leaned into her and kissed her.

Their embrace held. Clint wanted to turn away, wanted to jump in on the action, wanted to scream, and wanted to run. Instead, his gaze locked on them.

Beth's hands came up to Dustin's bare chest, urging him to end the kiss.

Clint sensed his reluctance as he tried to hold their lips locked until finally succumbing to her unspoken request.

"Dustin, it's time for you both to go." Her hands went up to Dustin's chin. "Please. You both made this an incredible decade birthday for me."

Her eyes never drifted back to Clint. Clearly, she wanted Dustin, not him. Or so she thought. He knew what she needed, knew what desires hid under all that control.

"This is ridiculous. We all want more. I can sense it. And now you and Clint want to stop it, as if nothing ever happened." Dustin turned back to him. "What the fuck is up with you?"

Clint felt an old fury awaken and clamp onto everyone of his muscles. "We fucked up. No sex with announcers. A simple rule. You ignored it. Now, what do you think will happen?"

"You need to chill out." Dustin scowled at him.

"Too fucking late for that." Clint needed to calm down fast, or he might say more than he wanted.

"Get a hold of yourself." Dustin stood up. "What the hell happened to you in that shower?"

"I got my head straightened out, that's what. We work with her. Everything has changed because we couldn't control our dicks."

"I'm still in the room, Clint. We *all* had a part in this. I'm not innocent here." Beth's voice stung him.

"Don't listen to him, darlin. He gets things in his head."

"Like what?" Beth looked straight at Clint.

Time to get the upper hand, just the way he liked it.

"No one can blame you, Beth. I don't."

"What do you mean *blame me?*"

"We were brought into the station to improve ratings."

Her eyes widened. "You think that I let you into my bed to save my job."

Clint felt like a complete prick, but that didn't matter. Regaining his discipline, his restraint, and his leverage was all that concerned him now. Best not to say another word. Make her sweat. So, he sent a shrug.

Beth swung her legs to the opposite side of the bed. She stood up with her backside totally exposed, then walked to the closet. Pulling out a baby blue robe, she wrapped it around her like a suit of armor. "Both of you, get the hell out of here."

"Darlin, please. Send him away, but not me." Dustin turned back to Clint. His eyes inflamed, furious.

"Please, both of you, leave. This went way too far."

"Okay. I'll leave with Clint." Dustin jumped off the bed.

"Thank you."

"This has been an incredible birthday. Neither of you nor Clint can deny it."

"Go. Now. Please." Beth's eyes glistened but no tears fell.

Clint felt like a thousand screws twisted into his gut, anchoring him to shame.

* * * *

Dustin hadn't said a single word since leaving Beth's apartment. The quiet as they drove to their rental house gave Clint time to think, to plan a strategy.

No more three-ways. No more morning show trio. No more Beth.

But Beth Taylor's fate on the show might prove more difficult when it came to persuading Dustin to Clint's side. Dustin might be a hard sell, but Clint never failed to get his friend back on plan, even with Dustin's well-known stubbornness set in.

As Clint parked in the driveway, Dustin broke the silence.

"What the fuck is wrong with you!"

Dustin's venom surprised Clint. The norm for Dustin ran from happy-go-lucky and jovial to, at very rare times, slightly agitated. But tonight, he sped past his norm to blazing fury. Clint needed to be calm, or his buddy might go into a rage.

"Dustin, we took things too far with Beth."

"What a pile of horse shit. Something happened back there. I felt it. I think Beth felt it, too. But I doubt you felt anything."

A storm brewed inside Dustin, a storm Clint didn't want to but must face. His plan for their careers demanded it. So, he pressed on.

"I'll tell you exactly what you felt, your hard dick in Beth's tight pussy. Nothing else."

"Fuck you."

"Something did happen. We crossed the line, and that complicates things at the station. We broke our rule." Clint chose his next words carefully. "She's a good announcer, but we have a team. Luckily, it's not too late to fix this mess."

"You and your rules can fuck off for all I care."

"Dustin, we are a duo. That works for us. Sure, she's been doing well for the past few weeks, but can she keep it up?"

"Clint, you can forget it."

"Forget what?"

Dustin's eyes narrowed. "Plans you have of deep-sixing Beth."

"She can't stay on mornings with us. It won't work."

"The hell it won't."

A pain exploded at the back of Clint's head. The dream of making it to New York and burning up the airways with Dustin seemed to be evaporating. Beth succeeded in wedging herself between him and Dustin over the past few weeks. Clint should've suspected it, but instead he remained quiet, enamored with her, too. She was a smart woman, but he couldn't let Beth win. Though he'd been stupid to let her stay as long as he did.

"That's Candi's decision, not mine."

"You can cut the crap. I know you. I know how you operate. If you have your way, she'll be knocked off the show in a month or two."

More like Monday morning.

"If she'd been producing numbers that pleased the owners, we wouldn't be here."

"She's got talent."

"In the bedroom, yes. On-air some, but not enough."

"Much more than some, and you know it." Dustin's hand clamped down on Clint's shoulder and delivered a vise-grip of pain. "I want her on the show. Period."

"Not possible."

"You fuck with her, you're fucking with me. Do you understand?"

Clint had never seen him so resolute about anything. The flexible friend he'd known morphed into an unflinching opponent.

"Dustin, can't you see what her game is? She's pulling our fucking strings and you're falling for it."

"You're the one who likes being the puppet master, not Beth."

"Really? When have we ever disagreed about the direction of a show?"

"She's innocent in this. She's done everything perfectly. Adding her to the mix forced us to be better at our jobs, pushed our limits, and the show has burned white hot. Hell, Candi told us what that survey found. What I don't get is why you're so adamant of getting rid of her with your love of high ratings."

"Because she doesn't belong on my show."

"*Your* show? Fuck you, Clint." Dustin unbuckled his seat belt. "She stays. End of discussion."

"That's not for you to decide. You and I agreed a long time ago that I make the decisions about what's best for our career as a duo."

"Keep talking, and you'll be managing a solo career."

"You don't get it. She's manipulated both of us. I can prove it."

Dustin opened his mouth to say something, but instead he turned and got out of the car. He slammed the door shut, and the car rocked.

He'd never seen Dustin so pissed.

Clint stepped out onto the driveway and closed the door with a more appropriate push.

"Best not to try me on this. You leave Beth alone, or you'll be the one off the show."

Before Clint could respond, Dustin marched up to the condo, unlocked the door, pushed it open, and pulled it shut with a loud boom.

Clint stood alone, looking at the door. What the hell could he do to change Dustin's mind about Beth? She'd trapped Dustin with her body. Clint had barely gotten free of her web.

That's it.

The plan formed in his mind. He must prove that Beth was not the innocent that Dustin thought. She'd been calculating on the battlefield, launching teasing sparks that ignited both he and Dustin, giving her the advantage. How could he have missed it?

Well played, Beth.

Still, Clint doubted that she'd ever faced an opponent like him. Tonight, he would fight fire with fire, with an ambush. He kept the tools that he needed in a black leather bag at the bottom of his closet, safely locked away.

Clint smiled, imagining how Beth might resist his education, but her body's reaction earlier had portrayed her deeper desires. She would react to the pain and pleasure he'd dish out. Her mind would race, her heart would pound, her pussy would ache…as her mettle to resist crumbled, bit by bit, under his guidance.

She'd willingly go to another time slot after tonight.

Clint walked up to the closed door, opened it, and entered. No sign of Dustin in the living room or dining room. Clint went to the hall. Surprisingly, Dustin's bedroom door was open.

Clint considered trying to talk to him again, but decided against it. Instead, he walked to the opposite end of the hall from Dustin's bedroom into his. He opened the closet door, grabbed the black bag from the floor, and brought down the video camera from the shelf.

He needed proof to show Beth wasn't an innocent. He'd get her to confess that she'd been working to split them up from day one, even if it took all night.

Chapter Nine

In her robe and slippers, Beth continued pacing as she'd been doing ever since Dustin and Clint left. She'd screwed up by letting the two hotshots into her bed. Now, Clint thought she'd only done it to keep her job, like she was some kind of whore.

She'd hoped that teasing them would keep them interested, but when they turned up the heat, she melted.

Oh God, how can I fix this?

She passed her wit's end thirty minutes ago. A pounding on her door jerked her from her thoughts.

"Open the door, Beth." Clint's voiced boomed.

"Are you serious? At this hour?" Beth put her eye up to her peephole. His face came into view. He seemed to be staring directly at her through the tiny eyelet.

"Let me in, now."

"Why should I? You made your point very clear."

"Don't make me bust it down. I will. You won't like the punishment I'd give you for disobeying me."

Beth's mouth went dry, but her want grew.

She unlocked and opened the door.

"Come in, but only for a minute."

"You like giving orders?" He carried a bag and a video camera. "That's about to change."

Her guilt rose in her throat. Had seeing her with Dustin enraged him? Could that have been the reason he'd lashed out so strongly?

This was first time she'd actually been alone with Clint since they met.

"So, why are you here?" The words came out sharper than she intended.

"Do you want to fight me, Beth? Give it all you've got."

"What if I do want to fight you?"

He smiled. "You already know how that will end."

"What's with the camera?"

"You'll find out soon enough." He turned away from her toward the dining table.

"And the bag?"

Rather than answer, he sat the bag down, shielding its contents from her.

"Hey, what's in that thing?"

"You really want to know?"

"Yes."

Clint turned back around. He held something behind him. In a split second, he spun her so her back hit his front, pulling her arms toward him.

"What the hell, Clint?"

His large hand covered her mouth. Confusion slashed her logic to bits.

Beth felt something on her wrists. Clint handcuffed her. Panic scraped her insides raw.

"These are leather cuffs. They lock together. You won't be able move your arms, so don't try. No talking, unless I tell you to. Nod to let me know you understand."

She nodded, her heart thumping full tilt.

"Beth, I know what you really need, and I will give you pleasure like you've never known before."

His words ignited something inside her that caused her body to respond.

He untied her robe and slid it down to the handcuffs. She heard a snap. The feel of the leather left her wrists for a second, and her robe fell to the floor. He snapped the cuffs back together, restraining her again. The cold air hit her exposed skin, causing her to shiver violently.

With anyone else, this would've been torture, but not with Clint. She felt hunger and guilt. He must've come back because he'd sensed her wicked desire for this treatment earlier tonight.

Clint's hand left her mouth. She heard him pull more items from his bag but dared not look back.

"You've been very bad, Beth. You drove a wedge between me and Dustin."

Tears welled up in her eyes. She deserved anything he wanted to dish out.

"Clint, I—"

His hand covered her mouth, again, forcing her to silence.

"I told you, no talking. You said you understood. I guess you lied, or intentionally disobeyed me. Either way, you will be punished."

Beth trembled. Desire rose up in her.

"I'm going to ask you some questions now. You can answer one of two ways, 'Yes sir' or 'No sir.' Do you understand that?"

Every syllable threw more coals into the lusty fire inside her.

"Yes, sir."

"Good. Have you experienced bondage before?"

"Yes, sir."

Only once, with her ex. She'd enjoyed it and wanted to experience more. He didn't.

"Interesting. *Lifer*?"

"What's a—Ouch!"

Clint pinched her nipple hard.

"You didn't listen to my instructions, Beth. Yes sir or No sir. That's it."

She held back her tears. "Yes, sir."

"Better. Definitely not in the lifestyle. I think you played around a time or two with some asshole who didn't have a clue about what real dominance and submission is. Right?"

"Yes, sir."

"I do know how to dominate. You want to learn more about that?"

"Y-Yes, sir."

"Listen to me closely. I will not repeat this. With me, you won't be experiencing some pseudo-bondage game. You will be restrained, blindfolded, gagged, and whatever else I deem necessary to train you into the bottom I know you are. You won't talk, taste, speak, move, or even come unless I give the order. You will obey every command I issue you without question. Do you understand?"

"Yes, sir."

"Did you and asshole have a safeword?"

"Yes, sir."

"Everyone thinks they know BDSM. Bullshit. You will have a safeword with me, but you also need a safe signal because you'll be gagged most of the time."

Oh God, I'm really going through with this.

"I will give you a way out of the incredible pleasure I can deliver, should you choose to end it. But understand this, when you do, I'm gone. Forever."

Her heart sank. She couldn't imagine never seeing him again, but hadn't that been what she'd wanted all along?

"Snap your fingers for me."

She did. Even with the cuffs, she could snap her fingers.

"Good. Now that I know you can, all you have to do to end your training is to snap them at any time. That's it. Once done, it's over."

"Yes, sir."

Clint slapped her ass with his bare hand. It stung like fire. She squeezed her legs together.

"I didn't ask a question for you to respond to. Wait until I do. Understand?"

"Yes, sir."

"Say, *Lobster.*"

"Lobster."

"That's the safe word. When you're gagged, snap your fingers. When you're not gagged, use the safe word. Understand?"

"Yes, sir."

"I don't think you'll end this session, but you might be too weak for what I have in store for you. If not, you'll have to prove it to me. Understand?"

Beth nodded.

She felt him grab a fistful of her hair and jerked her head back. "I told you that you only have two responses you could use. A nod wasn't one of them. Let's try again. Understand?"

"Yes, sir."

"Excellent. That's your last words for now, Beth."

Clint stood behind her. She wanted to see his face, wanted to let him know that she hated how badly she'd treated him.

He held something out in front of her. "This is called a ball gag."

Beth studied the red rubber ball with two long black straps attached to each side.

"Open your mouth wide."

* * * *

Clint couldn't get over how compliant Beth seemed to be. He'd expected her to resist, to argue. But she hadn't. Instead, her eyes showed so many emotions that he couldn't keep his head straight.

He pushed the ball in her mouth until her jaw widened, just enough to be slightly uncomfortable but not too painful.

"That's good, Beth."

He watched the subtle ways she rubbed her legs together, trying to feed her ache, and it drove hot lust down into his dick.

"Next, I'm going to show you how sensory deprivation can be quite an aphrodisiac."

He pulled out the blindfold and placed it over her eyes. He watched her shiver. He traced her curves with his fingers and watched the gooseflesh pop up along the way. She inhaled through her nose deeply.

God, she got to him.

He focused on the reasons he came here. One, pleasure her in the way he knew she needed. Two, extract the confession that she'd intentionally worked her way between him and Dustin in order to try to save her job. Third, get her to agree to another time slot.

That was the plan, and he must follow. He fortified his resolve to not deviate.

Clint guided her to the couch, leaning her over one of its arms so that her head rested on one of the seat cushions and her ass pointed up for his paddle—one side hard for serious punishment, the other with faux fur for a softer touch.

He brought out the leather ankle restraints and latched Beth's legs together, immobilizing her. She looked amazing.

"You've been bad, Beth." He patted her ass gently with his hand. He loved seeing her flesh shiver from his touch.

In his other hand, he held the paddle. He wanted to see her backside turn bright red, to watch her respond.

"So, I'm going to punish you. I don't want you to show any fear. You're gonna take it like the strong woman I know you are. Nod your head if you understand me?"

She did.

His entire body hardened with desire for her.

A virgin to his ways and yet she acted so bravely. It floored him. God, this wasn't how he thought this would go, but he couldn't stop now. He pressed on.

He started with the hard side first to render her ass hot. The first smack, Beth jumped. He loved this, loved her reactions. Another smack of paddle to flesh, she moved only a fraction. Each subsequent slap, she stirred less and less. By the seventh time, she didn't move a muscle.

He knew he shouldn't touch her tenderly just yet, but he couldn't resist. His grazed her reddened backside with his lips, then moved them up to the curve in her back. He kissed her there, took in a breath to pull in her scent. His already-stiff cock felt like it might burst.

"Remember, you can't come until I give the order."

Clint pulled her up to a standing position, and unlatched the ankle restraints.

"We're going to your bedroom now. I want you spread-eagle for me with that hot, tight cunt of yours ready for my cock. Understand?"

She shuddered, then nodded.

He guided her to the side of her bed to a sitting position, arms still behind her.

"Don't move."

He went to the other room, stripped out of his clothes, grabbed his bag and video camera, and returned. He'd never seen a more beautiful woman than Beth. Her breasts heaved with what seemed to be anticipation of what pleasures he'd bring out in her. Her pussy glistened with lusty dew. Everything about her pleased him.

Clint placed the camera on the dresser, and turned it on. He gently caressed her chest. Touching her soft skin thrilled him. He moved his hands to her nipples and squeezed them hard. Beth gasped and settled back. Her head tilted ever so slightly.

"That's it. Go with it, Beth."

She responded so deliciously. Her muffled moans called to him.

"Time to get you in position." He helped her to the middle of her bed and guided her back to the mattress. He tossed her pillows to the floor. Her bed didn't have posters, so he fastened braided nylon ropes to Beth's wrist and ankle restraints on each of their D-clamps. He took the loose-ends of each rope and tied them to a leg of her bed, stretching her out spread-eagle.

He tamped down his own excitement. His pleasure would come later, after hers.

Clint brought out a ten-inch dildo from his bag of tricks. He placed it on her naked stomach.

"Beth, this will hurt some."

She gave a defeated whimper.

"That's right. Let go. You don't have to do a thing but let your body respond."

He guided the tip to her slit, and he loved watching her wiggle as if trying to suck it into her pussy.

Clint took off the gag. She let out a long breath.

"Wiggle your jaw for me, Beth. It'll help those muscles relax and make you feel better. You're doing great."

Her cheeks turn bright red. Electric desire surged through him.

Clint thought about removing the blindfold, but knew Beth would get more out of the experience if she couldn't see.

"You have my permission to tell me what you want me to do with this big dildo."

"Yes, sir."

Holy fuck, she got to him. "Tell me, Beth."

"I want it inside me."

"I think you deserve that."

Clint got the bottle of lubricant out of his bag and slicked up the dildo. He pushed it between her swollen folds, stretching her.

"Remember, don't come until I say you can. Understand?"

"Y-Yes, sir."

Clint prodded the dildo in and out of her pussy, going deeper with each stroke. "Do you like this?"

"Y-Yes, sir."

"You want to come, don't you?"

"Yes, sir."

"Not yet." Clint intensified his pounding of her mound with the dildo. He reached up and tweaked her berry-like nipple. "Like this?"

"Yes, sir."

A fine layer of glistening moisture decorated her skin. He leaned down and lapped up a taste from her neck. She tasted sweet like honey. Clint moved over her.

"Would you rather have this dildo inside you or my pulsing cock? Speak freely."

"Yes, sir. I-I want your cock inside me."

"That's the right answer. You are a fast learner. I'm proud of you."

Clint pulled the dildo out of her and set it aside.

Without hesitation, he drove his cock into Beth's pussy. He needed to see her eyes, see her response. He pulled the blindfold off of her, and she flinched at the light.

Clint was mesmerized by her hazel beauties, as her pupils narrowed, clearly trying to focus. She smiled, and his heart leapt up into his throat. Master became slave.

Clint continued pistoning between her swollen folds. "Tell me how bad you want to come, Beth."

"Yes, sir. I want to come. I need to come."

"You can do better than that. Make me believe you."

"P-Please. I have to come. I can't hold back." Her body began thrashing underneath him.

"I can't let you, unless you tell me more." His own release loomed to the surface. He couldn't hold back much longer, but he wanted to make this moment last.

"Please let me come."

Now Clint felt the rush to the finish line. He lengthened his strokes into her cunt. He hoped that Beth reached new heights of sexual gratification and abandon.

His balls exploded hot liquid up his shaft. "Come for me, Beth. Do it."

"Y-Yes, sir." He felt her body shivering against him, loosing herself to her orgasm.

The walls of her channel clamped down on his cock, and he unloaded inside her.

Chapter Ten

The sleepy afterglow faded as Beth felt the restraints being removed from her wrists and ankles. Opening her eyes, she saw Clint. He brought feelings out of her she didn't know were possible. Thinking about how she gave herself totally to him moved her to tears. She wanted him, needed what he could give her. At the same instant, a pang of missing swept over her for Dustin. He should be here. She thought about saying so, but Clint hadn't given his permission for her to speak yet.

He turned to her and smiled. "You're awake. Good."

His sexy voice ignited nerve endings on her skin.

Clint leaned down, pressing his mouth to hers, soft and warm. His delicious tongue urged her lips to part, and she consented. As their kiss deepened, sparks zoomed inside her body. He'd been able to calm her mind and her worry by teaching her to let go. He'd stretched her, pushed her, and now he surprised her.

He sat up. "Beth, sit up for me."

Without hesitation, she did.

Sliding off the bed, he stood up, giving her a better view of his naked, muscled frame. Clint reached under her and scooped her up into his arms. "I want to take a shower with you, sweetheart."

Sweetheart? Her heart pounded wildly in her chest. He'd never said anything so wonderful to her.

Beth leaned into his rock-solid chest, savoring the feeling of safety he provided her. He carried her into the bathroom.

"Where are your towels, Beth?"

She couldn't find her voice. Had he given her permission to

speak? When she looked into Clint's eyes they showed he understood her hesitation.

"Sweetheart, no rules now. Trust me. You can be yourself now."

"O-Okay. The towels are in the hallway closet. I don't have enough storage here, and since it's just me, who cares. I suppose I should move to a new place. I've been here for so long, though. It's home. Oh God, I'm rambling."

"Not talking must've been very hard for you." Clint laughed. The sound elated her. "Stay put. I'll be right back."

When he walked out, she missed his presence instantly. She turned to the mirror. *Oh God.* No makeup, Medusa-like hair.

Clint's voice interrupted her inspection. "Let's get you cleaned up."

He held two white towels and her robe. He placed the towels on the sink counter, hung the robe on the hook. "How warm do you like the water?"

His tenderness caught her off guard, causing her to hesitate.

"I like it pretty hot, but not scalding," she stated, finally locating her voice.

Clint turned the faucet's handles. Water streamed out of the spout. His long fingers tested the liquid. "I think you'll like this temperature then."

Clint turned the middle handle and water streamed from the showerhead. Standing up, his hand pushed gently on her back and steered her into the tub. He followed her, pulling the curtain closed. The warm water hit her chest. It felt amazing. Clint pressed his front to her backside. She watched as his muscled arm appeared in front of her. He took her shampoo bottle from the bathroom caddy.

"Lean in and get your hair wet for me, sweetheart."

She felt his dick hardening against her skin. A river of longing snaked from her mouth, breasts, stomach, and thighs, down to her pussy. Beth stepped forward and let the water soak her head. The smell of water and strawberry shampoo filled her nose.

Clint's hands intertwined with her hair. He combed the strands with his soapy fingers.

"That feel good, Beth?"

"So very good."

Next, his fingers massaged her scalp, easing away every care. She tilted her head back into his chest. He laughed. She'd never known him to be so relaxed. That pleased her.

"Okay, lets rinse your hair now."

His hands never left her head as she leaned in. The water felt wonderful. His fingers wandered through her hair like an army, back and forth, from scalp to the end of her long strands, until all the soap was gone.

"That felt great, Clint. Thank you."

"I'm not done. I see your conditioner, and I'm gonna use it. Your hair is too gorgeous not to. Besides, I don't do any job half-assed."

"So I've learned."

Beth closed her eyes again as Clint deftly applied the moisturizing rinse. Each pass of his hand through her hair took her higher.

"After I finish, there's more in store for you. I'm gonna lather your body up with shower gel and get you nice and clean."

A shiver of excitement and anticipation zigzagged over her skin. She squeezed her thighs together as the ache grew in her channel. The man had come twice tonight, could she expect him to come a third time? Still, he was only thirty. Beth smiled at the thought.

Clint stopped stroking her hair. "God, you are an incredible woman, Beth Taylor."

"And you, Clint Moore, are an amazing man."

Beth felt his teeth clamp onto her ear. He cupped her breasts. Her nipples jutted out hard, eager.

"Soap up your loofah for me, sweetheart."

Beth obeyed, grabbing the loofah and the body soap from her caddy. She popped the top open and started to clean her neck.

"I'm doing that. You're here to enjoy, that's all."

His right hand left her chest, and she gave the soapy sponge to him. A wonderful dizziness took hold of her as one hand gently kneaded her chest, and the other lathered her back.

"You body is so sexy, smooth." His voice deepened, filled with what sounded like fathomless lust. Need tugged at her pussy. She wanted him to fuck her again. His cock, fully erect, pressed between her ass cheeks. Beth wiggled against it, hoping to urge him to increase his pace.

"That's it, Beth. Get that body turned on."

"Take me, Clint. I'll do anything to have you inside me."

"Yes, you will." He tweaked her nipple, and she thought she'd pass out from the pleasure.

His soapy hands firmly massaged her shoulders. The tension knots of the past few weeks released. Next he rubbed her neck, then he caressed the full length of her arms. Beth felt his hands move to her breasts, gently soaping them up. She thought he took his time washing her before, but now his pace crawled like lava from an ancient volcano. Clearly, he enjoyed lingering on her chest.

Beth wanted this shower to last forever. No one had ever treated her to such wonderful touches.

Clint crouched and began working on her lower body. His hands moved together, first on her right leg, putting a match to the fuse of her desire. She wanted him to touch her pussy, needed him to tease her backside ring. Then he moved to her left leg. Up and down, stopping just short of touching her mound.

"Clint, are you trying to drive me crazy? If you are, it's working."

"Good."

His stokes lengthened, and his fingers grazed her swollen folds. "Time to move to your hot cunt and tight ass."

His fingers meandered over her pussy and backside. Currents of desire shot up her spine from his wicked manipulation. Then, his fingers danced against her clit. A jolt rocked deep into her channel. Her control fled, and her wildness swelled.

He stood up. "Time to rinse, sweetheart."

He turned her full circle, washing the conditioner from her hair and the soap from her skin. Beth felt so clean and turned on.

The water now hit the back of her legs. His cock moved ever so slightly, most likely to the beat of his heart pulsing.

Then Clint went back to his knees. He grabbed her ass and brought her forward. Beth felt his warm tongue laved her clit, setting her whole body to throbbing.

What an amazing mouth.

Clint moved his tongue over her tender folds, his hands still pulling her in tighter, closer. Every cell inside her seemed to be tingling, moving, burning. His fingers kneaded her backside's flesh while his mouth worked her over.

The ripples of pleasure became crashing waves of explosive ecstasy.

Beth's orgasm washed over her as Clint continued tasting her pussy.

"O-Oh."

Her vocalization seemed to urge him on more. His tongue pierced her, advancing into her channel.

Her back arched. Tears spilled down her cheeks as the rapturous release consumed her. Her legs wilted. She rocked against his mouth for what seemed to be several minutes.

When her orgasm finally subsided, Beth stroked Clint's head. He looked up at her, eyes full of lust.

She smiled. "What about you? You need to be cleaned up, too?"

He sent her a wicked grin, stood up, and handed her the loofah.

Beth aimed the stream at Clint's chest. The water cascaded down his impressive frame, soaking all of him. She marveled that the liquid didn't turn to steam once it touched his smoldering skin. Elated that she'd get to touch him and please him, her stomach jumped.

She pointed the showerhead toward the tiles, dropped to her knees, and spent extra time on his lower half. His hard cock danced in front of her waiting mouth. With one hand, she washed his balls. With the other, she tried to circle his shaft, but its large girth prevented her fingers from touching her thumb. Beth looked up. Clint's eyes never left hers.

Beth leaned back to let the shower's spray rinse Clint's entire body. She leaned in and licked his cock from base to tip.

"That's it, sweetheart. Clean me up with that hot mouth of yours."

She swallowed him as far as she could go until his dick hit the back of her throat. Clamping her lips, she felt Clint's cock pulsing. Pleasuring him increased her want to a frenzied state. Her insides boiled hot.

"Fuck. That feels so good."

Pushing his buttons, feeling him respond from her treatment increased her thirst. She slipped her mouth up and down his hard dick, faster and faster. Beth kneaded his balls.

"That's it, Beth. Fucking perfect."

His cock jerked in her mouth. His orgasm must be close. She vowed to swallow every drop of his hot liquid.

His body went rigid and he grabbed a fistful of her hair.

"I-I'm coming!" Clint yelled.

His warmth exploded in her mouth. She sucked it all down.

When Beth felt Clint's body slacken, she released him.

"That was incredible, sweetheart."

Beth licked the tip of his cock and watched him shake from his afterglow.

He pulled her up and kissed her.

When their mouths parted, their eyes locked on each other.

"Clint, I think I could fall in love with you."

Why had she said that to him? It wasn't like her to be so impulsive.

Her heart plummeted to the floor when Clint dropped his gaze.

* * * *

Beth's body still buzzed from the weekend with Clint and Dustin.

When they all came together the first time, Dustin and Clint fell asleep in minutes, but Beth's last climax thundered inside her for more than an hour, keeping her deliciously awake. As exhaustion took her to dreamland, she let herself imagine them staying the whole weekend. She definitely could get used to the kind of treatment they gave her.

What a birthday. She marveled at all that she'd done that night. Her first threesome. Sex with Dustin while Clint watched. Later, Clint teaching her submission, and then the amazing shower with him. Her time with them had left her so satisfied and spent.

Beth could still feel them in her pussy. She'd never felt so alive.

For a moment, Beth wondered if Clint regretted their time together. But he sat quietly and watched her make waffles, rather than hightailing it out the door, so she doubted it. He took three bites and drank some coffee. How could a man say so much in the bedroom and behind a microphone, but be so non-verbal everywhere else? Still, he smiled at her and kept squeezing her hand. Words held very little meaning next to that.

He and Dustin made her feel so sexy. The birthday blues were long gone, but she wasn't sure what was left in their place.

Clint had left an hour ago with the promise to call her tomorrow to set up dinner with him and Dustin. *Dinner with two helpings of delicious man-desserts.* She grinned.

Her lips and nipples were dry and sore from all the incredible kissing and sucking. The remaining aches reminded her of how many times they'd entered her and brought her to orgasm. She still couldn't believe that she'd actually let herself go. Clint and Dustin amazed and surprised her. She'd never been so satisfied. The two studs gave her the best gift a woman could ask for. Complete, passionate abandon.

Ring. Ring.

Her cell jolted her from her thoughts. Where had she left it? The living room.

Beth jumped up and put on a robe.

Ring. Ring.

By the time she got to the phone, she missed the call. Beth looked down at the screen.

Candi?

Why would she be calling her on Saturday morning? Was the weekend announcer sick and the boss needed a fill-in?

She hit the dial button, and it went straight to voicemail.

"Candi, this is Beth. I saw you called. Give me a call back."

Beth didn't really want to talk to the boss. If the woman had any idea of what happened last night, Beth would be toast. But the guys would never tell. Of that she had no doubt.

Whatever Candi wanted, Beth vowed to not let it ruin her mood. Last night had been unbelievable, and she wanted the feeling to continue.

However long Clint and Dustin worked at the station, she'd be okay with it from now on. Really *okay* with it. She even suspected that when the two finally moved on to some bigger and better station, and they would, she'd be very sad.

* * * *

All weekend, Clint felt Dustin's mood turning darker with each hour that Beth didn't call them back.

After he left Beth's apartment, they'd planned on getting together for dinner with Dustin. It never happened. Though both he and Dustin had left several messages, Beth never returned them. No voicemail. No email. No text message. Nothing since he'd left her.

Sunday, he and Dustin went to her house and knocked on her door. No answer.

Had Clint crossed the line with Beth? Pushed her too far? He wanted to comfort her, and let her know how much being with her meant to him. All he could do now was make sure that she and Dustin stayed on the morning show. They'd be an incredible duo together. His jaw clenched tightly at the thought of moving on without them, but that would be best for all of them.

Late Sunday night, he and Dustin sat in the living room, willing the phone to ring.

"You gonna say something?" Dustin's tone sliced razor sharp. "Anything at all?"

Clint wanted to tell him about his time alone with Beth, but he couldn't. Dustin wouldn't understand his attraction to bondage. If he told him, it would just be another nail in the coffin of their already-crumbling friendship. His gut wrenched at the thought. Best to leave it be.

"If you won't bother to answer me, then don't fucking talk to me." With that, Dustin went to his room and slammed the door shut.

Once he got to Candi tomorrow morning, everything would be okay.

But everything wasn't okay.

* * * *

At four a.m., Clint and Dustin jumped into the car. Clint hated the drive. Dustin kept an invisible barrier between them ever since they left Beth's apartment Friday night. Now, Clint sensed it growing with each passing minute.

When they got to the station, the only person that could tear down Dustin's blockade was missing. Beth. Could she just be running late? The latest she'd ever come in last week had been four, and that day she stopped to pick up some breakfast burritos for everyone.

Fuck.

Fruitlessly, Dustin dialed her cell over and over just as they had done all weekend. No answer.

Clint looked for the hundredth time at the digital clock in the studio. *Five-thirty a.m.* Still, no Beth.

His mind swirled with memories of being with Beth and Dustin on Friday night, of watching the two of them fuck from the bathroom doorway, of restraining her to the bed for his taking. No one compared to Beth.

His recalled her soft body, her submission, her kiss, her response to the things in his black bag.

"Damn it." He'd left his bag and the video camera at her place.

Clint felt completely lost. Next to her, his self-control that he always trusted failed him. He had turned off the camera, erased the little he'd recorded, never asked her to confess. Her body confessed enough for him, and he believed that showing Dustin any video of her divulging the truth would do nothing but drive him further away from Clint.

Could he fuck things up any more?

Two of the most incredible people he'd ever known. Beth, so beautiful, intelligent, soft and determined. He wanted her to be some typical, washed up, wanna-be announcer, but she wasn't. He'd never met a more talented broadcaster or wonderful human being. Sometimes he could swear, she saw through all his bullshit. And Dustin, so strong, confident, loyal and real.

What would he do once he found out Clint had gone back to Beth's apartment and ravaged her? Clint hoped he would never find out.

Amazing sex, yes, but in the light of day all that disappeared. And what was left? Regret. And boy, was he feeling that now.

By fifteen minutes to air time, Dustin darkened to a pitch black.

"Dustin, maybe Beth's in the break room. Take a look, will you? If not, there's a phone there. Try her again."

He glared back at Clint, but did exit the room.

Clint hated the ruse, but he needed to get Dustin out of the studio. He needed to talk to Candi privately.

When Dustin was out of earshot, he punched the speaker button that went to the control booth. "Ted?"

"Yes?"

"Is Candi's home number posted in there?"

"Sure is."

"Can you get her on the line for me, ASAP?"

"No problem, Clint."

No problem. Nothing could be further from the truth.

A minute later, Ted poked his head out of the control booth. "Candi's on line two."

"Thanks."

Ted asked, "Everything alright, Clint?"

"No, it isn't." He worried that Dustin might walk in and hear what he would say to Candi. He only had a few minutes, at best.

Ted waved and shut the door behind him.

Clint headed to the chair that Beth claimed the very first day, but he couldn't bring himself to sit in it even though it was the closest one to him. Instead, he went to his chair. Line two flashed red on the receiver. He punched it.

Candi just couldn't have—not over the weekend. She couldn't be that cold.

"Candi, this is Clint."

"Why are you calling me at this hour?" Candi's voice sounded agitated and then changed to concern. "Something wrong at the station?"

"Yes, everything is wrong at the station."

"What's happened?"

"Beth isn't here. I tried to call her an hour ago. No answer. Dustin and I left her messages all weekend, and she never called us back."

"Really?" Candi didn't sound surprised.

"What did you do?"

"I let her go."

"You what!" Clint yelled. His body turned ice cold.

"I canned Beth like we agreed." Candi sounded smug with a hint of confusion.

"Over the weekend? Why were you in such a goddamn hurry?" Despair gripped Clint's entire being. He'd expected Candi to pull Beth from the show today, not over the weekend.

His plan had been when Candi showed up at the station to tell Dustin and Beth that he needed to talk to her after their shift about some promotional ideas. The next step would've been to tell the woman that he didn't want Beth off mornings. In fact, he would insist that Beth stayed with Dustin. Then he'd give his resignation. Candi firing her over the weekend had destroyed his plan.

"Clint, I don't understand why you're reacting this way. You and I discussed this. In fact, this was one of your terms to come here. At any time you didn't feel like she was contributing to the show—"

"I know what my fucking terms were. They've changed."

"Well, I wish I had known. But based on what you and I talked about in my office, I executed on that."

Clint could tell by her tone she didn't give a damn about him, Beth, or anyone. A cold-hearted bitch to the max.

"Where exactly did you *execute* Beth? Did you have her come into the station over the weekend? You could've let me know."

"I told her she could pick up her things any time this week. She told me she'd come by sometime today."

"You told her over the phone, didn't you? Very classy." Fury and guilt seized him. Candi was right. She acted on what he'd demanded. Get Beth out of the picture. But the picture had changed.

"You've got to calm down," Candi said. "This is what you told me you wanted."

"What reason did you give her for letting her go?"

"I told her the truth. You and I talked, and while we thought she had talent, we want the show to go in a different direction. I offered her the midday slot, but she turned me down. I also told her that I'd give her a great recommendation."

Fuck. Beth knew what he'd done. She likely hated him for it. He hated that she knew and hated himself for what he'd done.

"Clint, what do you want me to do?"

"I want you to get Beth back. I want you to tell her that I changed my mind and that I want her on the show. Convince her to stay, whatever it takes."

Dustin's voice boomed from behind him. "Who the fuck are you talking to?"

Clint turned and saw the rage in Dustin's green eyes.

Candi's voice filled with more patronization than he'd ever heard before from her. "That isn't possible. Just calm down. When I get to the station, you and I can talk."

"You better make it possible, Candi, or Dustin and I are out of here."

"Candi. You had her fire Beth. You fucking asshole!" Dustin planted a solid punch on Clint's face.

Pain exploded in his jaw, and he stumbled back from the blow. He dropped the phone and nearly fell off the chair. He didn't care. He deserved even more than Dustin dished out.

Ted rushed in. "What the hell?"

Clint heard Candi's voice. "What's going on?"

He picked up the receiver and slammed it as hard as he could on the cradle. "Fuck you, Candi."

"Fuck you, Clint." Dustin growled, then charged out of the room.

Clint's grandfather's voice clawed at the inside of his head. *Yool always be worthless, boy. A firefly caught in jelly jah. All flash, no future.*

* * * *

Beth looked in the mirror. Her eyes looked swollen and felt like tenderized meat. She'd tried to stay in bed, but her internal clock denied her that luxury. Too many years on the morning show.

She'd been tempted to turn on the radio just to hear how Clint and

Dustin would explain her absence.

What an idiot.

Of course they'd say nothing. That's how it worked in broadcasting. When someone got canned or moved on, the station treated it as if they'd never been there. If any listeners called in asking about the missing announcer, which rarely happened, they were told that the announcer had moved to another job, whether true or not. For Beth, it would be the same. As if she'd never existed. The last ten years would evaporate into nothingness.

She choked down a sob. She'd cried more than enough since Candi's call. Beth took a dampened washcloth and put it up to her eyes. The coolness of the cloth eased the sting. No makeup today, not that she ever wore much. No place to go.

But losing her job wasn't what hurt the worst. Knowing that Clint was a part of it broke her into a million pieces. What a fool she'd been.

"Beth, I've okayed it with the higher-ups to offer you the midday shift." Candi actually sounded sympathetic.

For a split second Beth had been tempted, but then she thought about Scott Davis. He currently worked that shift at the station, and he didn't have a contract like Beth's. Scott would cost the company only two weeks of severance as opposed to Beth's buyout of twelve months. Though Beth wasn't sure what she would do, she refused the bitch and quit, which cut her severance package in half. She just couldn't be ruthless like those assholes Clint and Dustin.

"Candi, you know what you can do with that offer?" Thankfully, she kept the waterworks at bay until after hanging up the phone.

How long had she cried?

She wasn't sure. But the sobbing ended, leaving her eyes swollen.

She'd let those two jerks into her house. Did they know that Candi was jettisoning her off the show? Beth wasn't certain about Dustin, but she was about Clint. He'd been unusually strange that night, until they got horizontal. *Asshole.*

Who to blame but herself? She'd let them in. Pushed her boundaries past any known place she'd ever been before. And now, what did she have? Nothing. She'd lost her show, her job…and her heart. Why did she take that jump? She wasn't someone who took risks. That's why she stayed all those years in a medium-sized market station. What the hell was she going to do?

God, she'd really lost it.

Since they left, she'd not left her apartment. She ate the rest of the chocolate ice cream. No help. She tried to start working on a resume. No luck. She started to call the damn duo but stopped. She would not give them the satisfaction. No way.

The two assholes had kept trying to reach her. She refused to answer any of Dustin's or Clint's phone calls, knocks on the door, text messages. Whatever their version of the truth, she didn't want to hear it. Ever. She didn't want to ever see them again.

She felt so alone. Isolated. She needed her bearings. Needed a new place, a safe place. Nancy, an old friend, managed a station in Albuquerque. They'd talked shortly after Candi's phone call. Nancy would hire Beth, for the overnights, not mornings. What did it matter? It was a job, a place a washed-up announcer could escape to.

BANG! BANG! BANG!

"Beth, I know you are in there. Let me in." Even from the other side of the door Dustin's voice sounded loud, firm, and with a dose of, what, concern?

She shook her head to clear her mind. She needed him to leave before she did something stupid—again.

BANG! BANG! BANG!

She threw down the washcloth and walked to her front door. "Go away."

"No. I am not going away. I have to talk to you."

Could Dustin really not have been part of getting her off the morning show? She looked at the time on her cable box. Six-forty. Why else would he be here instead of at the station?

It didn't matter what his reason for being here was.

"Go back to the station. You have a show to do."

"Fuck the goddamn show!" Dustin shouted. "You've gotta believe me, I didn't know."

She did believe him. But did that matter? She wouldn't let him in, couldn't let him in.

She'd let Dustin and Clint into her house, the invaders of her safe world. They'd touched her like no other, not just body to body, but deeper. That scared her to her very core. She hated vulnerability, but like it or not, she was vulnerable. If she opened the door for Dustin, she wasn't sure what she might do. *Start crying again?* That would be horrible.

No. He must leave.

"Just go away, Dustin. I don't want to see you."

But she didn't mean it. Couldn't mean it. Everything inside urged her to open the door and…what? Run to his arms like a starry-eyed schoolgirl?

She hated how much she wanted him, needed him.

"Beth, please. Take a chance. Open the door." His voice was softer.

Her will evaporated. So much for wisdom coming with age. More than likely she'd regret it, but she opened the door.

"You have two minutes to explain, cowboy. That's it."

"I only need two minutes, darlin." Dustin walked in, closing the door behind him.

"That's all you got, and the clock is ticking."

Dustin moved closer. "Clint's an asshole. Candi's a bitch. I promise you that I didn't know anything about it."

He spread his arms wide, moving in very close.

Her thoughts whirled with a myriad of emotions. Her fear of trying to find a new job demanded attention. Her confusion about her night with Clint and Dustin demanded attention. Her desire to melt into Dustin's muscled chest demanded attention. But what boiled to the surface shoving those thoughts aside was a single prevailing emotion, fueled by Dustin and Clint's betrayal. Rage.

She stiff-armed him and pushed him away. "Bullshit. You've been with Clint for years now. You know his methods, his style."

"I swear—"

"He must have done this before. I can't be the first announcer he's removed."

Dustin's eyes shut tightly, which let her know the truth. Clint had done it before, and Dustin had seen it.

She continued, "What did you think would happen? He would change? Well, he didn't. You didn't. Grow up, Dustin. You've been playing Mr. Innocent to Clint's Mr. Badass too long. How many lives have you two left in rubble? You are just as guilty as he for all the damage you've done. And you both played me like I was some silly teenager."

"Beth, I promise you that—"

"And then you screwed me, tossed me to the side like yesterday's trash."

Dustin reached for her, but then pulled back. "It's not like that, Beth."

"You're lying to yourself, Dustin, and you lied to me."

"What can I say to make you understand, darlin?"

"Don't call me that anymore. Do you understand that?"

"Beth, just give me a chance."

Part of her wanted to, but the other part would not be denied. She felt like she was sinking deeper into emotional quicksand. Dustin must leave.

"I gave you two minutes. Now get out."

Beth heard Clint on the other side of the door.

"Guys, please. I can fix this. I can."

Dustin's face went red hot. In what seemed like a single choreographed movement, he flung open the door, pulled Clint inside, and pushed his shoulders to the wall.

"Clint, you fucking idiot." Dustin's face turned bright red.

"I am," Clint agreed. "But I can fix it."

"How?" Dustin said through clenched teeth. He didn't release Clint, but kept him pinned against the wall.

"In our contract, we have the right to bring on any talent we want." Clint's eyes darted back and forth from Dustin to hers. "And we both want Beth, right?"

"Go on," Dustin spat.

Clint's words came fast. "Well, we demand that Beth be brought back. If they refuse, we walk. All three of us. Corporate won't let that happen. Candi will have to cave."

Did Clint think he could fix everything by triangulating their boss into a corner? Was that his game? Manipulating everyone to whatever he desired?

A renewed fury stormed inside Beth. "Candi already caved, Clint. She caved to your demands, then fired me. Like you wanted all along."

Though Clint still remained pinned to the wall by Dustin, he turned his head toward her. "Beth, that's what I wanted, but not anymore. I promise."

Beth so wanted to believe him, but what did it matter? Candi would only take her back by an act of coercion. She could never settle for that. She did have some pride left, though she'd been so foolish with these two.

"Fuck you, Clint. Fuck both of you."

Chapter Eleven

Beth watched Clint wince as if she'd slapped him.

"Please, I can fix it. I swear I can. I'll make it up to you. To both of you." Clint's shoulders slumped.

"You betrayed me. You knew Friday when you came to my house."

"I didn't know that Candi would do anything that fast. I thought I could get to her before…" His gaze dropped.

"But you did know. You knew what you said to her. When are you going to stop lying? This had to be in the works since you first got here."

Clint groaned. "Yes. Until I got to know you."

"But you didn't do anything about it. Candi called me Saturday, right after you guys left. Can you imagine how that made me feel?"

"Yes, but…"

Dustin hit the spot to the left of Clint's face, putting a crater in her wall. "I ought to beat you to a bloody pulp."

"Yes, you should," Clint answered.

"What do you want from me?"

"I want the show to continue—with you and Dustin."

"But you've lied to me and even to Dustin. Why? Why didn't you tell us until now? What is it with you and all your secrets?"

"I don't have any secrets."

But she could tell by the way he answered that she'd hit some mark. Clint had his own demons. Could those monsters be the reason he'd lashed out at her? At everyone? Why he pushed everyone away?

Dustin shot out, "The hell you don't."

"I told you the truth. I want you to stay on the show. There are no secrets."

Clint's last words rang false to her.

"You're lying. Tell us both. What is it with you?"

"I didn't tell either of you Friday night about talking to Candi because I thought I could talk to her before she canned Beth. I had no idea that the bitch would act so quickly. But believe me, I can fix it. Just trust me."

Clint turned his eyes away from Dustin's stare, but he didn't try to break Dustin's hold. She'd explored their bodies when the three of them had made love and she had no doubt that they were equally matched in the strength department. So why didn't Clint push back? It didn't matter. Everything changed since their night together when everything had gone so perfectly…except for that one moment.

The moment when Dustin touched Clint's shoulder.

Beth's stomach flipped as the thought of what Clint's secret might be took hold of her. It made sense as to why he'd tried to get her off of mornings.

"Clint, you really want me back on the show?" she asked.

"I swear it. I really do."

"What changed your mind?"

He looked confused, trapped. "I think that you can make the show explode in the ratings."

"So it is only about ratings?"

"Yes. What else is there?"

"And you and Dustin will be on mornings with me?"

"Yes."

"Liar!" she yelled. "You only want you and Dustin to succeed. I am just a roadblock to that plan. You've knocked other announcers to the curb to achieve what you want."

She saw she'd hit a mark when Clint winced. "That's how I used to feel, but not any longer. I want to get you two set up, and then I'll resign."

Dustin's face darkened. "What the fuck are you talking about?"

"It's for the best." Clint's face filled with what looked to Beth to be fathomless suffering, very old and recently unearthed.

She shouldn't care, but she did. Seeing him in such pain bore into her like a ten-inch drill. She hated how he suffered. The fear in Clint went deep, and it clouded everything in his life. She knew the power of fear too well. Though her way of handling it differed from his, the end result for both of them produced paralysis.

No matter how hard it would be for Clint to face his demon, Beth couldn't let him live another day shackled to it as she had to her own.

"What do you really want?" She thought she might already know why. But what if she was wrong? What if it was something else?

"I want you to be on the show, Beth. I wish I could convince you."

So she continued. "Is that all?"

"What do you mean?" Clint asked.

"Do you want us to have sex again? The three of us?"

Clint answered, "Of course."

Beth softened her delivery. "You liked my body?"

"Yes."

She spotted his cock growing in his pants. She was on the right track.

"Kissing me?"

"Yes."

"Tasting me?"

Dustin turned to her. He looked confused, but his face showed that desire filled him just like Clint. And with each word, the fever inside her increased. She would take the risk, push past her own paralyzing fear—for Clint.

His eyes filled with lust. "Y-Yes."

"Fucking me," she breathed. Get him hot. Off balance.

"I loved fucking you," he growled.

"But something happened that night, something that scared you."

"I don't know what you mean, Beth." Clint's face darkened.

She hit the crux of his pain. It scared her. The old Beth would've stopped, fearing what might be set free. But the new Beth refused to stop. At Clint's age, she'd turned down an offer for the top station in LA. Why? Fear. And her dream vanished away. For her that dream would never be realized. But for him, it wasn't too late. His desire boiled at the surface within grasp. She wouldn't let him miss his chance. Clint, who seemed completely in control on the outside, fought nightmares every waking moment. She'd make him face the truth, no matter how painful, but not alone. He'd given her something amazing, unlocking her hidden desires. Now, Clint needed her and he needed Dustin.

"When Dustin touched your shoulder? Do you remember?"

Clint's eyes had a storm swirling underneath his calm.

"I remember that." Dustin turned toward her and nodded.

Did he suspect the truth? She wouldn't be surprised that he would be *okay* with it. Dustin was the kind of man who would be all right with just about anything. But she wasn't sure if Dustin would take the chance. His decision, not hers. But Clint must at least take the chance. Beth knew how horrible regret could be.

"You seemed to turn to stone. Why?"

"I don't remember that."

"But you do."

Clint's face went bright red with anger and fear. "Either you let me fix things or you don't. I don't give a damn."

It killed her to see him suffer so much. How long had he carried this secret? How awful it must be. She shouldn't care, but she did. Their lovemaking was more than just sex. She saw Clint's walls come down for a moment. He had been open, if only for a few moments.

She pushed on for Clint and for herself. "But you do give a damn. Why else are you here? And you do remember, Clint. Tell us the truth. What's your secret?"

* * * *

Clint did remember, but he could never tell them. Never.

Why was Beth so insistent? Why was Dustin? This wasn't what was supposed to happen. Clint had his reasons. They couldn't know them. Not the real reasons. Ever.

"I don't know what you are talking about." The lie stuck in his throat like a hundred tangled fishhooks.

"But you do, Clint." Beth sat down on the sofa where he sat last Friday night when everything began to spin out of control. "Dustin, let him go."

Dustin obeyed her and stepped back.

Clint slumped forward away from the wall. Instantly, he missed Dustin's hands on his shoulders. A pitfall loomed on the path should they continue this line of talk.

Gotta keep my head.

Beth patted the middle cushion where she'd reclined between him and Dustin. "Clint, please come sit next to me."

But he didn't move to the sofa. Being that close to her, to her body, to her softness would loosen his resistance. Every one of his muscles seemed to contract like a vise. He needed to get her off this line of talk. Get back to what he'd come here for. Make things right. "None of that matters. We need to be back together on the morning shift. Let me fix this, Beth." The desperation to convince exploded inside him rocking the very crux of his being. "I can do it. I really can."

"But something has been troubling you, and it isn't about Candi or the station. It's something else, something you've carried for a long time. And I think that you came close to letting it go last Friday. Didn't you?" Beth's eyes glistened brightly, revealing the sincere concern she had for him. "Aren't you tired of all the lies? Don't you want to stop hiding, Clint?"

Beth's words were like truth serum entering his blood stream, urging him to answer. *Oh God.*

"I don't have anything to hide." Clint swallowed hard to keep the truth down.

"You can trust us," Dustin stated. "We're here for you."

Clint wanted to trust them. But he couldn't. They wouldn't understand. No one ever could. Hell, he didn't understand it himself.

Tears fell from Beth's eyes. Tears for him. "How long have you carried this burden?"

Did she really see through him, through his facade? The memory of his grandfather's scorn resurfaced.

The feelings inside him that he'd been able to keep under control rattled against their chains. These two were tearing at the ancient metal. Chunks of his control gave way.

"Please, won't you come sit down next to me?" Even more tears streamed down her cheeks.

Her unshakeable kindness left him unable to resist her command, and he joined her on the sofa as instructed. That was as far as he'd let her take him. No further. No matter what spell she had over him, he must resist. Clint clenched his jaw tightly.

I have to keep my mouth shut.

Beth put her arms around him and squeezed. He wanted to run, to scream, to wrap his arms around her.

"What happened to hurt you so deep, Clint?" Beth's tone softened.

Clint had never been able to rely on anyone except himself. How he wanted to trust her. He really did. Their night together opened up old wounds in ways he'd not felt since that night so long ago. But trust wasn't a luxury he could afford. Since thirteen, he'd been on his own. Depending on no one but himself. That had been Clint's *modus operandi.* It was how he survived.

And how had that worked out for him? Until he met Dustin, he'd been alone. But even after their friendship deepened, Clint held himself back. Not allowing Dustin to know him fully. His plan had been to tie them together permanently with a spectacular career. The sex they enjoyed sharing women had been an added benefit. Clint had navigated that course for several years, walking with scissors—but not running.

The last several weeks with Beth had knocked him adrift. His and Dustin's intense desire for her had been clear from the moment they met. And as he'd gotten to know her, his longing grew. He'd been unable to get his head around what to do with that. And now, she shined a bright light into his darkest places.

Fuck.

Dustin sat down on the other side of him. "Trust us both. Nothing you can say will ever change how I feel about you. Nothing."

"Me either," Beth added.

"I'm not so sure about that." Everything would change. Just like all those years ago. And he would be alone, again. Clint couldn't bear the thought.

"Believe me, buddy." Dustin's arm came around Clint's back, interlocking with Beth's.

Sitting between these two amazed him. He leaned back into their arms. Why had he been running so long from that awful night? Their touches were gentle and comforting.

Could he take the risk of sharing his memories? Hell, he'd worked hard to bury them away all these years. Why dig them up now?

"No matter what you say, it will be okay." The tenderness in Dustin's voice cut through Clint's defenses like a warm knife through soft butter.

Beth grabbed his hand and squeezed. Dustin mirrored Beth and took Clint's other hand.

At that very moment, it happened. Clint believed. Believed in Dustin and in Beth. And he trusted them like he'd never been able to trust anyone, not even himself.

The walls he built around his grandfather's scorn crumbled.

It all came out. The old pain. At first through clenched teeth, in choked sentences. "I was only twelve when I went to live with my grandfather..." Then, stronger as buried rage clamored to the surface.

* * * *

A car accident killed his mother, father, and infant brother.

His other siblings, three younger sisters, went to live with his mother's only sister in Florida. She told Clint that she just couldn't take on another mouth to feed. His aunt had two girls of her own. She also told him that she didn't have any knowledge on how to raise a boy.

His aunt patted him on the head like he was a dog right before he got on the bus that would take him from his home in Portland to the man he'd only seen in pictures on his father's nightstand.

"Clint, you're twelve years old. You're practically a grownup. You should understand."

But he hadn't. How had he been able to choke back the tears when he stepped up on the bus? He waved at his sisters through the window as they were shepherded into his aunt's car. Once out of sight, the tears fell until he finally drifted off to sleep in his seat on the bus.

Clint was sent alone to his only living grandparent, James Thomas Moore, twenty miles from Interstate ninety-five on the border of New Brunswick and Maine. It took less than a half-day after Clint's arrival for him to realize he was nothing more than free labor to the old man. His grandfather was a man of very few words. And Clint's loneliness grew. Try as he might to win the man's approval, that never happened. Especially after that one night.

Clint was thrilled when a teenage boy, a year older than he, came to work for Clint's grandfather for the summer.

Clint's room had two twin beds. His grandfather motioned to the teenager to take the free bed.

"Nevah too early to learn to share, boy."

Clint was thrilled with the boy's arrival. They became great friends over the next few weeks. The teen gave Clint's grandfather a secret nickname—Mr. Ruff Ruff. It meant, all bark and no bite. The sadness of losing his parents and the loneliness of being away from his sisters faded in the company of the boy.

Everything changed the night of Clint's thirteenth birthday. No gift, cake, or even acknowledgement, though his grandfather knew what the date meant.

Clint and the boy were sent to bed right after dinner. Mornings always started hours before the sun came up.

"Happy birthday, Clint." The boy's words and smile pleased Clint.

It rained, and though it was early summer, the temperature was cold. The threadbare blankets weren't able to keep Clint warm. The teen suggested that they double up their blankets so they both could get warmer.

The boy smiled at Clint. "That's how the cowboys kept warm on cattle drives."

"Really?" Clint asked.

"Yep."

Hormones ignited inside him. He touched the boy's shoulder. They stared at each other, leaned in and kissed.

* * * *

Clint put his hands up to his face. The memory of that night overwhelmed him.

"What happened, Clint?" Beth touched his shoulder.

"My grandfather caught us kissing. He jerked the boy up out of the bed, and told me to stay put. I heard my grandfather beat the boy. When the screams died down, my grandfather came back alone. He glared at me. Then told me to go to sleep before slamming the door."

"What happened to the boy?"

"From my window, I saw him walking to the road. I wanted him to look back, but he didn't. I never saw him again. Two months later, I left for Portland and never returned."

Beth choked out, "My God, you've carried that all these years."

He never shared any of that with anyone. And while telling them, tears flowed out of his eyes like a dam bursting. He felt the salty tracks they left on his cheeks. He felt like he'd run a marathon.

"What happened to that fucking grandfather of yours?" Dustin spat out. "I'd be happy to take the old man out."

"Too late, Dustin. My youngest sister found me about two years ago. She called me the day before his funeral to tell me the old man died."

"You were only thirteen when you left for Portland." Beth's eyes were bright red and tears fell freely from her eyes. "Did you have other family there?"

"No. I could pass myself off as eighteen. That's when I got my first job in radio. I worked overnights at a little station."

Dustin looked at him. "You've been carrying that for a long time."

"Yes."

Beth moved in close, her face inches from his. She kissed the tear remnants on his cheeks. "So, is that why you froze when Dustin touched your shoulder?"

"Yes." Clint felt like a deflated balloon.

"You were scared that Dustin would realize you're in love with him?"

Chapter Twelve

"Yes, I'm in love with Dustin." Clint finally said it out loud.

Had he made a mistake?

It was one thing to tell his tale of pain, but another to admit to the secret of his love for Dustin. Clint feared how Dustin might react.

He didn't expect reciprocation sexually. He'd seen Dustin's skill in the bedroom. He didn't believe that his friend's tastes ran to the man-on-man variety. Clint also didn't expect an equal return emotionally, though he and Dustin had been close for years. Would his admission of love end their friendship? Clint's gut seized into a knot.

"I thought that might be the case." Dustin's stare pierced his very center.

That he suspected astonished Clint. "You did? How long have you known?"

"A while," Dustin nodded, "though you should call me dense. Before Friday night with Beth, I was never certain."

"Really?" Clint couldn't get his head around it.

Dustin smiled broadly. "Yes."

"And you're okay with that?" A lump grew in Clint's throat.

"I'm more than okay with it. Friday night blew me away. But I promise, tonight will be even more incredible." Dustin squeezed Clint's thigh tightly.

Heat shot into Clint's already lengthened cock from the Dustin's touch. Beth leaned in and kissed along Clint's jaw. Her hand went to his other thigh. A rhythmic thrum grew inside him. As he moved in closer, Clint could feel Dustin's hot breath on his neck. It sparked all the nerve endings on his skin to life down to his cock.

"I understand why you two might want to console me, make me feel better. My story is tough to listen to. But I don't expect that. Besides, Dustin, I doubt you've ever—"

"Don't bet on that." Dustin shook his head. "I don't have much experience, but I did have a couple of semesters in college where I experimented with just about anything offered. One guy offered quite a bit."

Clint thought the admission would've been a shock to him. But it wasn't. Dustin's *bring-it-on* attitude was part of his charm. But a college fling was just that—*a fling*. It would be best not to move forward, especially if Dustin only considered this as a kind of intervention therapy for a friend. The thought stopped him cold. Down this path heartbreak was inevitable, and he'd had his fill of that.

"Clint, please don't be afraid." Beth squeezed in closer.

Did she wonder if he'd only been with her Friday so that he could get close to Dustin? That wasn't true. Clint desired Beth. Everything about her bewitched him, and he'd fallen completely in love with her.

She helped him accept his *other* desires. Passion for a man's muscled touch on him—Dustin's touch. He wanted both of them and in the most sinful of ways.

"I know what it's like to be afraid." Beth leaned over Clint and took Dustin's hand by the wrist.

He craved them both. But at what cost? Though Dustin said that tonight would be incredible, what did that mean? A night in the sack, followed by a sunrise of regrets?

"You two don't have to do this."

"No, we don't. But we want to do this." Dustin leaned into him. "And Clint, most of all, I want to do this because I want you to be happy for once in your life."

A flood of euphoria washed over Clint. He could no longer resist Dustin and Beth.

"Do you trust us?" Beth's eyes sparkled.

God, she amazed him. "Yes."

Clint's heart pounded against his ribs. For years, that memory of his grandfather jerking up the boy from his bed imprisoned Clint. He'd been running from himself for so long. He cut off half of himself ever since he left that farm. Now, he purged the old bastard from his mind with the help of these two incredible people, willing to explore with him the other half of his sexuality.

Beth lifted Dustin's hand and guided it to Clint's bulge. Dustin squeezed Clint's dick through the fabric of his pants. Something akin to a lightning bolt ripped through Clint.

"We're really going to do this." Clint looked from Beth to Dustin.

Both their eyes danced with lust. Then Clint looked down at Dustin's shorts and spotted his rock-hard cock.

"Yes, we are definitely going to do this." Dustin's mouth enveloped Clint's earlobe, sending rivers of hot lava through him.

Clint's arousal exploded to the stratosphere. "I'm not sure what to—"

Dustin interrupted his sentence with a full-on kiss.

Fireworks erupted down Clint's spine, as Dustin went deeper with his velvet probe. Inviting. Different than with Beth. Stronger. More urgent. Manly.

Clint forced his eyes to stay open as their making out deepened. Dustin's eyes closed. Tears flowed from Clint's eyes when he finally shut them. The depth of passion from their kiss demanded it.

When they ended their kiss, Dustin looked down at him, green eyes sparkling like an Emerald Island spring. But the lusty storm behind those orbs permeated into Clint, stirring up his own passion to a fever pitch.

Then Beth came into his view, smiling. "You both are amazing."

She saw through his deception and made him face his darkest fear.

"Beth, you're so incredible, so sexy." Clint put his hand at the back of her neck and pulled her in for a kiss.

Sweet lips. Soft. Wet. Delicious. Feminine. He went deeper into her, his tongue drilling. No holding back. No fear. More desire flooded into his already boiling body. For the first time in his life, he gave free rein to *all* of his desires. And being free energized him.

Continuing their mouth play, Clint moved his hands to her round breasts and pinched her nipples through her blouse. She let out a moan that pleased him in ways he'd never experienced before. His entire body juiced up.

Beth broke their lip lock. "God, you kiss so good. Kiss him again, Dustin."

Dustin took Clint's mouth hostage. Ten thousand volts of raw lust poured into him over conduits of lips and tongues.

Dustin unbuttoned Clint's shirt while deepening their kiss. The coolness of the room didn't offer any relief to the heat building inside of Clint. Letting himself enjoy the moment of freedom, he moved his hands over Dustin's t-shirt and explored his muscled chest. Clint stopped at Dustin's nipples. He pinched them, drawing out a long sigh from the hunk.

The kiss broke, and Dustin smiled back at him. "Beth, help me get Clint out of his clothes."

Beth nodded. Her fingers went to his belt while Dustin eased him out of his shirt.

"So, I'm the only one that is going to be exposed here?" Clint gave them both a wide grin.

"Serves you right after Friday night." Beth laughed.

"For now, yes." Dustin teased. "But not for long."

Beth eased his zipper down and curled her fingers around his boxers' waistband. His cock vibrated against her touch. She pulled the fabric down, releasing his dick. Her thumb circled the head. Intense pressure built up in his balls.

A sudden shock blasted through his body as Dustin's mouth latched onto his left nipple and sucked hard. He closed his eyes tight against the onslaught of desire. Then Beth's mouth slid down the full length of his cock. Their oral pleasure blasted him beyond every boundary, transporting him to want and longing.

"Feel good?" Dustin asked, coming up for air.

"It feels fantastic."

"You think that's good, just wait." Dustin grinned wickedly.

He patted Beth on the shoulder, and she stopped sucking on Clint's dick.

He wasn't sure what Dustin planned, but he would go the distance.

Then Dustin leaned down and encircled Clint's dick with his large hand. He bent down and licked the tip of his cock. The *rightness* of being with Dustin and Beth only added to the desire that took him over.

"You like that?" Dustin asked.

"I love it."

Dustin smiled at him and then swallowed Clint's dick to the base. A tsunami of emotions ripped through Clint. Juicy heat combusted inside him. Nothing else existed except this moment with Dustin and Beth.

Beth gasped. "Does it feel incredible, Clint?"

"Yes."

Then her lips covered his. Her tongue brought responses that charged up his body even more.

As Clint enjoyed the two mouths working him over, he recalled the moment he froze when Dustin touched him Friday night. What a fool he'd been. No more. This miraculous duo were taking him on the ride of his life. He never wanted to exit.

Clint touched Dustin's hair, probably the only thing soft on the man.

Dustin looked up at him. "Do you want to come this way?"

"Yes, but not now. I want you both out of your clothes."

"As you wish." Dustin smiled.

He and Beth were out of their clothes in seconds. Dustin's cock jutted out, demanding attention. Clint knelt down in front of him, but then a fit of trembling took him over. He couldn't move. Could the old bastard still be in his head? *Fuck.* Clint closed his eyes tight, trying to will himself free of old demons.

Beth knelt down next to him. "It's okay, Clint. Relax. I'll help you. For now, keep your eyes closed."

She put her hand over his and guided it up to Dustin's dick. Together, their hands encircled his thick cock . Clint could feel the pulsing.

"That feels so good." Dustin's voice came out like a growl.

Beth instructed, "Open your eyes, Clint. And look at what you're holding."

He complied. Dustin's cock danced in their hands.

She continued, "All that hardness should tell you how much he wants you. We both do. You have nothing to fear here. You're safe with us."

The paralysis of Clint's body left as his renewed desire pounded inside him. He moved his hand up and down Dustin's cock. Liquid heat surged into Clint's dick.

"You wanted to taste him Friday night, didn't you?" Beth asked.

"Yes."

"But you denied yourself." Beth whispered into his ear. "But here's another chance. Just taste the tip. Don't go too fast."

Quivering, Clint obeyed Beth and his own lust. He licked the slit of Dustin's dick. It tasted salty on his tongue. Dustin moaned, delighting Clint.

Beth urged Clint on with her lips against his neck. Sensations of electricity rocketed through him. He wanted to please Dustin and wanted to be pleased by him. The past would not hold him hostage any longer.

He swallowed the head of Dustin's cock. It filled Clint's mouth.

"Go slow. Relax your throat." Beth instructed.

Clint's passion wouldn't be harnessed any longer, nor would it wait for him to gain some quick expertise. Instead he clumsily took all of Dustin's meat down to the base.

"A little too much teeth," Dustin informed. "But please, don't stop."

Beth positioned herself between Clint's legs. "Whatever I do to you, you do to Dustin."

Her breath on his dick took him higher. With a slow exhale, she blew on the tip of his cock, driving him to wicked madness. Clint slipped his mouth off Dustin and began blowing on the head of his dick.

"Beth's a good teacher, but be careful, Clint. That will drive me wild."

Beth licked his shaft from the base to the head. She circled the cone with her tongue and then slipped back down to his balls. Every fiber of Clint's body shook from desire for her to swallow him whole. As before, he repeated on Dustin every touch and taste that Beth worked out on his dick.

Her lips amazed him. His release was building up inside him. By the way Dustin's cock jumped against his tongue, Clint believed Dustin's liquid would be shooting in seconds.

"Suck it. Suck it hard." Dustin yelled.

Beth slid her hot mouth slowly down Clint's dick. Shocks of delight spread down to his toes.

"That's it, Clint. You've got it." Dustin's hands pushed against the back of Clint's head.

His friend's cock seemed to be getting harder inside Clint's throat. His own dick, slick from Beth's treatment, writhed like a beast.

With each moment, Clint's skill increased as he mimicked what he experienced from Beth's mouth on Dustin's cock. He learned how to bring Dustin close to the edge by speeding his tempo, then stopping just before the man could come. After a few minutes, he could start the assault again. Over and over he repeated the process, bringing Dustin close to release before backing off. He sucked on Dustin's cock until his mouth and jaw began to ache, but he would not stop. He loved every bit of it. He loved the power and ferociousness.

Dustin stopped his lunging forward into Clint's mouth. "I can't hold back much longer. If you're not ready to swallow, then you better stop right now."

But Clint hungered to taste Dustin's warm liquid. So he increased his tempo up and down the meaty shaft, not stopping. Beth's mouth moved faster and faster on Clint's cock. Fervor whirled like a tornado as his own orgasm moved up his shaft.

He looked at Beth just as an orgasm took her. He loved hearing her moan with his cock in her mouth, watching her fingers rubbing her clit, feeling her face between his legs, slick with orgasmic sweat.

"O-Oh God." Dustin screamed as he shot into the back of Clint's throat.

Clint swallowed every drop. And then, his own delirium took him, as he shot his load down Beth's throat.

And for the first time in his life, he experienced true ecstasy.

Chapter Thirteen

Beth stood in her kitchen without a single thread of clothing. She practiced modesty even when alone, but after her time with Dustin and Clint, she enjoyed freedom like never before. Putting on a robe to make coffee and toast seemed ridiculous. She liked the feel of the cool air on her skin.

Her body ached from all the lovemaking with Clint and Dustin over the past several hours. She shivered at all they did to and with each other. Their appetites for her weren't lessened by their lust for each other. Instead, the more they explored each other, the more they wanted her.

She sent the bread into the chambers of the toaster. The smell of coffee in the maker wafted up to her nose. She looked over at the time on the stove. Six-thirty.

"Oh shit." The guys were late for their shift. Even being the hot announcers at the station, she doubted even corporate would tolerate a no-show.

She wouldn't go back to the station. Call it stubbornness or pride, she didn't care. After seeing Clint face his fear, how could she do less? She might land on her face, but she must at least try. Put an audition tape together and send it out. But how could she leave these two amazing men? They'd shown her more about herself then she ever dreamed possible.

She needed to leave. They had each other. Besides, she knew that they would leave her once the next big offer came. Better to get the jump on that.

Yes, it would crush her, but what else could she do? Get in deeper with Dustin and Clint? It was already more than she could handle. Another month or two with them and the heartbreak would split her into a million pieces. No way.

Last night must be their last time together.

She looked down at the tray with three cups of coffee, six slices of buttered toast, and some sliced fruit she'd prepared. If the guys were as hungry as she, this would not be enough fare, but it would be a start.

Beth walked in with the meal thinking she'd find the guys still asleep, but instead they were sitting up, and smiling at her. Their naked muscled chests looked wonderful. Sadly, her sheet covered their bottom halves.

"Hello, beautiful." Clint winked. "That smells great."

"I could eat a horse." Dustin's arms went straight up, and he let out a long yawn.

"It's not much," Beth apologized.

"It'll be fine, darlin.'"

"You know you guys are late for work." She placed the tray on the end of the bed.

Dustin didn't hesitate but took a piece of toast and devoured it in two bites. Clint took her hand and guided her back to the bed between him and Dustin.

Talking with a full mouth, Dustin said, "Like I said that first day we met, there are more important things than broadcasting."

Her stomach announced her own hunger. Forgoing manners, she consumed a piece of toast almost as fast as Dustin had. In less than five minutes, the tray's contents were consumed and they all sat drinking coffee.

An inconceivable sadness engulfed her. She couldn't bear giving over more of her heart to them, and that meant never having them in her bed again.

Dustin turned to Clint. "Shall we tell her?"

"Tell me? What?"

"Dustin, you have no social skills do you?"

"You're right about that." Dustin put his arm around her back.

His forearm and bicep enveloped her. She loved it. She felt sexy.

She tensed. Were they hoping for more nights with her? Lots of wonderful amazing sex until they got their next offer and left her in the dust? That could not be. She needed to let them know right now. Her heart couldn't bear anymore.

"Guys, there's something we need to get straight."

"Exactly." Dustin grinned broadly. "That's what Clint and I were just talking about."

Beth sat up.

"Dustin, slow down." Clint ordered. "Beth, we both want you."

Her heart leapt in her chest. She wanted them. But a few days, months, even a year would lead to only heartache. When they tired of her, she'd be alone. It would be too much.

"Guys—"

Clint put his finger on her lips. "Don't talk. Just listen."

Dustin began rubbing her neck.

"Okay."

"You are the most amazing woman that either of us has ever known. And we think that what we have together, the three of us, is also amazing." Clint kissed her shoulder.

"It's been great, guys." Tears welled up in her eyes. How could she tell them that it was over? But for her own wellbeing, she must.

"Beth, Dustin and I want to marry you."

"Yes, we do."

Marry? "What? B-But—"

"Just listen, honey." Clint kissed her shoulder again. "I know that's not possible legally, but we want you to be our wife."

"Darlin, you should marry Clint for the license, though."

"Why?" Beth tried to form a sentence, but couldn't.

"There are lots of reasons you should marry at least one of us." Dustin informed. "Benefits, taxes, housing."

"That is no reason to marry."

"That's true. The only reason to marry someone is for love. And I love you, Beth."

"You think you do, but this won't work. It can't."

"Beth, what are you afraid of?" Clint kissed her shoulder again.

She swallowed. "Say I agree to this. What about you two? Clint, you love Dustin and he loves you. I know."

The guys turned to each other and smiled.

"That's the reason it won't work." Beth felt her eyes fill with tears.

"You don't want us to love each other?" Clint took her chin and turned her face to him.

"Of course not. Your hearts are open to each other. That thrills me. But think. When you came out of the bathroom and found Dustin making love to me without you, how did that make you feel?"

"Beth, that won't happen again."

"That's easy to say, but you can't be sure."

"And Dustin, did you know that Clint and I had sex?"

His face showed surprise. He didn't know.

"We did. Great sex. Without you. How does that make you feel?"

He shrugged. "I'm okay with Clint touching you, with or without me."

"Of course you are. Nothing fucking bothers you. But me, that would bother me. My ex cheated on me. I found him in bed with my best friend."

"That's not us." Dustin shook his head.

"You can't tell me that you two won't have sex together without me. I couldn't ask you not to. I know I should be more evolved, more modern, but I'm not. I don't think I could handle it."

Clint grabbed her hand. "Beth, you're making excuses. I sense it."

"Maybe, but it doesn't change anything for us."

"Since your divorce, have you had a relationship with anyone?"

"What does that have to do with anything?"

"It has everything to do with why you're fighting something you know is rare. Love. You're terrified we'll break your heart. But you've already come too far not to be hurt."

Could he be right?

"Trust me, Beth. I know how to break the wall you've built up over the years."

"What do you mean?"

"You're so much stronger than you think. It may be a cliché, but love *is* worth the risk."

Dustin winked at her.

Clint stood up. "Do you trust me?"

"I do."

He pulled her off the bed. Her body quivered, not sure what he had in mind, but still very excited at the possibilities.

Clint turned to Dustin. "Bring in the dining room chair with the arms."

"What are you up to?" he asked.

"You'll see."

Dustin jumped from the bed and left the room.

Clint walked to the closet door. He opened it up and brought out three of her robes.

"These will work fine."

"What do you mean?"

He pulled the ties free from their respective robes.

Oh God.

He grabbed something from the floor and placed it on her nightstand. It was his black bag. He must've left it the other night.

Dustin returned with the chair.

Clint pointed to the corner by the window three feet from the bed. "Set it there."

Dustin did as instructed.

"Beth, get in the chair."

Trembling, she obeyed. Clint tied her left wrist to the chair arm.

"What the fuck are you doing to her?"

"Something I've done for years. Remember the time when Max told you that I'd been seen at that BDSM club?"

"I do. You denied it."

"I did. I lied."

"Fuck, Clint. What's wrong with you?"

"I never told you about it because I knew you'd react this way."

"How else am I supposed to react? This is fucked up."

"It isn't. Before Beth, it was the only way that I could get off with a woman. I liked the control."

"And you want to do that to Beth now?"

"I've come a long way with you and Beth helping me. Now, you need to open your mind up. So does she. She's got a barrier that needs to come down. We can make it come down. Together."

"I won't stand for her to be tied up. It's—"

"Beth, tell him." Clint's voice took on the commanding tone he'd used the other night.

Without a thought, she answered, "Tell him what, sir?"

"Do you want me to tie you up?"

"Yes, sir."

Dustin's eyes widened. Then she spotted something else in them. Lust.

"Would you like Dustin to tie up your legs?"

"Yes, sir."

"This is nuts." He sounded outraged and confused, but she detected something else, perhaps a hint of curiosity.

"Maybe, but if we can get past her fears, her life will be much better."

"Alright. I'll play along. For now."

"Good. You won't be disappointed."

Dustin tied her legs and Clint tied her wrists.

Clint leaned in and whispered. "Did you think we were going to fuck you in the chair? Wrong. You're going to watch Dustin and I fuck."

Her heart jumped up in her throat.

"B-But—"

Clint kissed her quiet.

She'd learned so much about herself from him. Could he be right that she could handle more?

Dustin looked at her, hesitation evident on his face.

"Are you sure about this, darlin?"

Beth nodded, but she wasn't sure.

"Okay. Clint, what do we do to her now?"

"Nothing. We're going to give her a show."

"You mean—"

"Yes. She needs to watch you and I have sex. It's the only way she can break down her barriers. Beth thinks jealousy will ruin a chance with us. I don't believe it."

"How far are we going with this?"

"As far as it takes." Clint turned back to her. "You remember our safe word?"

"Yes, sir."

"Dustin, you can end this too, should you chose. If Beth or any of us say 'lobster,' everything ends."

"I think this has gone too far. Maybe I should say it right now."

"Dustin, she needs this. You love her, don't you?"

"Of course I do."

"Plus, you and I need this. The oral you and I enjoyed last night was great, but there is so much more to explore. You experimented in college, but that was just experimentation. I have no experience at all. If the three of us have any chance of making this work, I think we have to try this."

"I really want it to work. I think the three of us have something incredible. It's just hard for me to see someone I love tied up."

Dustin loved her. Clint loved her. She loved them. But was that enough to make it work?

"Do you love me, Dustin?" Clint asked.

Instead of answering, Dustin walked over and planted a kiss on him.

Beth's insides flip-flopped. What if Clint's plan didn't work and her jealousy severed any chance of a future with them? So be it. She trusted him. One way or another, she'd see this through.

Clint took Dustin's hand and walked him over to her bed. The two muscled men looked amazing. Beth squeezed her thighs together. To end it, all she needed to do was say the safe word. Instead, she fixed her gaze on the two men about to make love.

They knelt on the bed, facing each other, their cocks touching. They kissed. Hands wandered over backs, chests, arms, legs, and asses. They pulled on each other, bringing each other closer, tighter.

Dustin dropped his mouth to Clint's neck and sucked. Beth felt shivers run up her spine.

A moan escaped from Clint. His pleasure added to her want. He cupped Dustin's balls.

Dustin leaned back. "Want to suck on me?"

"God, yes."

Dustin rolled onto his back, his dick fully erect.

Clint leaned down and licked the tip of Dustin's cock.

Beth smiled. She trained him well. Then the doubts rose up in her. Could she really handle this display? Clint thought she could, but she wasn't so sure.

She blinked as he swallowed Dustin's dick and continued fondling his balls. Dustin's eyes closed and licked his lips. The show reached into her, pulled at her. She loved seeing these men caring for each other sexually. They'd both been in denial. Clint was afraid of admitting his desire, and Dustin unwilling to see the truth. Now they both were free to explore and enjoy each other.

Could she be free, too?

Dustin began fisting the sheets. Clint's mouth must've been pushing him to scream out in pure lust.

"Stop, Clint. God, you're good at that. I want to taste your cock, too. How about a little sixty-nine?"

He nodded and positioned himself to comply.

From Beth's position, she could easily view all of it. Clint's oral care began again on Dustin's dick. Dustin looked over at her and smiled. Next, his lips slid down Clint's cock. A wonderful warmth curled inside her channel.

Dustin's hand reached around Clint's backside. She watched as the tip of his finger went between Clint's ass cheeks. Beth sighed. Her body couldn't stay still.

Their frenzy increased with each stroke on the other. Something rose inside her, something other than the jealousy she'd expected.

"Beth, you want to see more?" Clint asked.

"Yes, sir."

She wanted these men to experience the full pleasures they could give one another, to give themselves completely to each other…with or without her watching. Beth also knew that she wanted them together and alone. How hypocritical of her to expect something different from them when it came to her.

"Would you like to see us fuck each other?" Dustin smiled.

Clint turned to Dustin. They looked at each other, then back to her.

"Is that what you want, Beth?" Clint asked.

"Yes, sir."

He laughed. Then he turned back to Dustin. "I'm game if you are."

Dustin smiled and kissed Clint.

Beth's excitement grew, imagining how each of them would feel begin so connected to each other.

"Who first?" Clint asked.

"There's only one way to decide: rock, paper, scissors."

They both laughed, and Beth stifled her own giggle.

Dustin and Clint's fists went to their palms once, twice…the third time the result appeared. Clint formed his hand in the shape of paper, Dustin in the form of scissors. Being the winner, the cowboy donned a condom.

Clint reached into his black bag and brought out a bottle. He popped the lid open and squeezed some lubricant into his hand. "Lie down, Dustin."

Instantly, the cowboy fell back on the mattress, legs outstretched, cock hard and ready.

With his moistened hand, Clint stroked Dustin's cock, slicking it up with the lube. Then he reached around his own backside with his lubricated hand and circled his entrance. Beth watched as his index finger disappeared into him while his other hand stroked Dustin's dick.

"O-Oh." Clint moaned.

Beth's ached grew. She wanted more. Needed more.

Another finger went in. Then a third. All the while pumping Dustin's hard cock, which would take the place of his own digits.

Clint moved one knee over Dustin, straddling him. His ass hovered over Dustin's dick. Then he moved down over the tip of it.

Clint jerked back up. "I'm not sure that I can do this."

"Sure you can. Relax." Dustin began stroking Clint's dick. "Spread your cheeks wide. That's good. Now, just tease your hole with my tip, don't slip it in yet."

She watched as Clint followed Dustin's instructions.

"Perfect. Try to push down on it, just a fraction."

"Okay. I'll try." Clint's eyes closed. He writhed over Dustin.

"Yes. Feels so good."

When Clint's eyes popped open, she realized Dustin's dick had pierced past his ring. "It's in, Dustin. Your dick is inside me."

"Inside, yes. But there's more."

"I know."

After a minute, Clint started up and down Dustin's dick. Short strokes.

"Darlin, if he keeps this up much longer, I'm going to go crazy."

"Yes, sir."

Beth watched the thin layer of sweat build up on both men.

"Clint, how does it feel with my cock inside you?"

"Fucking amazing."

"Are you ready to take all of it into your tight hole?"

Clint didn't answer, but slid down until the full length of Dustin's dick went inside him. Beth watched Clint's back arch and his head tilt.

"Breathe. That pain is temporary."

Shortly, she watched as Clint's shoulders relaxed.

"When you're ready to let me take the driver's seat, pinch my nipples to let me know."

Clint nodded, but didn't move.

Shortly, Clint's breathing sped up. He looked over at her and smiled. Leaning down, he kissed Dustin. Then he sat up and pinched his lover's nipples.

Dustin didn't hesitate. Lifting his hips from the mattress, he sunk his cock into Clint backside.

"O-Oh God!" Clint's shout seemed to vibrate in her body.

Dustin continued his assault into Clint's body. Clint matched Dustin's strokes with his own up-and-down motion, faster and faster.

Beth imagined how every inch of Dustin inside Clint must've felt. Amazing. Stretching. Thrilling. When Clint slammed down on him, Dustin's balls jumped.

Over and over. Up and down. The show drove her wild. Her body buzzed, her want expanded.

"Dustin, I want you on top of me." Clint rolled off of him, and stretched out face down onto the bed.

Dustin climbed on top of him. "You ready?"

Clint fisted the sheets. "Yes."

Guiding his cock into his lover with one hand, Dustin held Clint's shoulder with the other.

"God, you're so fucking tight. Clint, if you want to drive me crazy, clench my dick with your insides."

Beth relished watching them make love. She would never tire of it. Ever.

"That's it, pardner." Dustin's voice resonated with excitement.

At first, Dustin's strokes were slow, then faster.

Clint's body responded. He rocked with him, stroke for stroke. The sight of them fucking each other charged her up. She writhed on the chair, her body hot with desire.

Beth couldn't help herself. "Deeper, Dustin."

"Listen to Beth. Fuck me hard."

Dustin's motion changed to slamming strokes. Deep. Hard. Powerful. Clint took all of him.

"I-I'm c-coming."

"Do it." Clint closed his eyes.

Beth savored the moment as Dustin came. Shortly, his body sagged, spent from his release.

Clint stared at her and smiled. "Don't pull out, yet. Let's both roll on our sides, so I can face Beth."

She got an eyeful. Clint's cock was still rock-hard. With Dustin's dick still inside him, Clint began fisting his dick. Dustin reached around and tweaked Clint's nipples. In less than a minute, white liquid shot out of Clint's cock. He turned his head back to Dustin, and they kissed again.

Her insides surged with sexual hunger.

She wanted them to express their love for each other, to fuck wherever and whenever, no matter if she watched or not.

Clint turned back to her. "I knew you could take it."

"Yes, sir."

"I'm not so sure," Dustin teased.

"What do you mean?"

"Well, she's not seen you fuck me yet."

"Later, I promise. First, I want to hear her say what she's really feeling. Speak freely, sweetheart."

"You can fuck each other all you want. But if you don't fuck me pretty soon, I think I'm going to explode in flames right here and now."

"Oh, really?"

"Yes, sir."

"Should we believe her, Dustin?"

"I think so."

"Would you like to see how she responds to my kind of expertise? You'd like it, I think."

Desire shot up inside her. "Yes, sir. Please, sir." She wanted more. Wanted them.

Dustin hopped off the bed. His hand moved up her thighs. "Tell me more about this, Clint. If she loves being dominated, I'm game."

Electricity pulsed through her. "I want you. I do."

"Did I say you could speak?" Clint barked.

"No, sir."

"I'll let that pass for now, but don't let it happen again. Understand?"

"Yes, sir."

Clint pulled out a vibrator from his bag.

"You have to earn this. If you do, I'll put it inside you, slow and easy."

"Okay."

"You spoke without being given permission." Clint winked at her. "Dustin, pinch her hard. You need to let her know that we expect nothing but her absolute submission."

He nodded and tweaked her nipples. The sensation felt amazing.

"Too soft. Make her really understand that she can't speak without our consent."

Dustin clamped down harder.

Beth winced, the pain mixing with intense pleasure.

He jumped back. "Sorry."

How could she make him understand? She wanted this, needed it.

"Look at her, Dustin. She's responding."

Good. Clint would help him, like he'd helped her to understand.

"Our dominance over her is about *her*, not us." Clint walked over and patted Dustin on the back. "We get her to go deeper into her sensuality, to let go of her logic, her control, and she gets to experience pleasure beyond her imagination. Look at her. That's our reward."

Dustin's gaze locked on her, his eyes showing he battled with the idea. How could she make him understand? She must depend on Clint to do that.

"Ask her yourself if you don't believe me." Clint switched the vibrator off.

"Darlin, do you really enjoy this?"

"Yes, sir."

Dustin smiled. "I can't deny how sexy you look tied up. I never thought I'd like such a thing, but I do. Watching you squirm on the chair drives me crazy. Okay, Clint. Lead the way."

* * * *

Previously, Clint had only trained women to be bottoms. Tonight, he enjoyed instructing Dustin in the ways of dominance.

He watched Dustin work Beth over, still restrained to the chair. The man was a natural Dom. Over and over, he demanded she beg him to fuck her. She obeyed quickly. No internal deliberation. Just complete abandon and desire.

Dustin's fingers circled her clit while his other hand tweaked her nipple.

"You've been very bad, Beth. Did you get off watching me fuck Clint?"

"Yes, sir."

A massive pulse of longing rushed through him as Dustin bit

down on Beth's other nipple. Clint watched her head tilt back in response. His dick hardened again.

He walked over and handed the vibrator to Dustin.

"Slip this into her. Get her good and ready for our dicks."

"Great idea."

Dustin eased the toy into Beth. She didn't utter a sound, looking so sexy as she bit her lip.

"You like this in you, darlin?"

"Yes, sir. I do like it."

"Beth, you broke a rule, " Clint informed.

She stared at him, her face filled with confusion.

"You will be punished for saying *I do like it*. Not something you've been given permission to say."

Clearly, Beth's shivers came from excitement.

"Punishment?" Dustin asked.

"Untie her."

"Then what?" Dustin released her ties.

"You're about to find out. Stand up, Beth."

Instantly, she obeyed him and stood up.

"Dustin, sit down in the chair and bend her over your knee."

"Okay, buddy." His cock stood up at attention.

Clint enjoyed seeing Beth's body draped over Dustin's lap. "Later, you'll get to use my paddle, but first, your hand will have to suffice. Get that ass nice and red."

Dustin began slapping her backside. Clint watched her lip quiver. She didn't make a sound. What an amazing woman.

Dustin slapped her cheeks until they burned bright pink.

Clint stroked his dick, excited, thinking about plunging it into Beth's pussy. "Beth, get on your knees, now."

"Yes, sir." She slid off of Dustin.

He stood up and walked in front of her. "Suck my dick."

She went down on him and pumped him with her hot mouth.

Clint took one of his vibrators from his black bag and gave it to

Dustin. "Tease her ass with this."

He took it, turned it on, and began working her over from behind. Clint could tell she liked the treatment as her lips tightened on his dick. Beth hiked her ass up to give Dustin better access.

Her eyes were closed. She looked amazing. Clint felt good, strong, protective…connected.

"Dustin, you getting her hot and bothered back there?"

"I am."

"Cup my balls, Beth."

She obeyed immediately. That pleased him.

He loved her touch, his softness, her compliance. "She's hot, isn't she, Dustin?"

"Yes, she is."

"Should we fuck her? I'm not sure she's ready yet. What do you think?"

Dustin's lust-filled eyes fixed on her naked body. "She's ready. Aren't you, Beth?"

Her mouth stopped her oral treatment on him. "Yes, sir."

Clint moved to the bed and guided her on top of him. Her swollen folds rubbed against his dick and electric heat rolled through him. "Dustin, eat her ass out, and get her ready for your dick, while I fuck her pussy."

Dustin dove down to her backside. Her soft, inviting body against his mustered more lust, more heat, more passion. Everything about her thrilled him.

She tilted her head to look at him. Her blue eyes bright and alive with lust. His body responded with sweltering hunger. He wanted to satisfy her so thoroughly, so completely that she would have to agree to be with him and Dustin.

Clint guided his cock into her mound.

"O-Oh."

"Go ahead, sweetheart. Say anything you want now."

"Thank you. Pressure. I love it."

"Tighten that pussy around my dick. That's it. God that feels good. You like what Dustin's doing?"

"Yes, sir."

He felt her tremble against his skin. "Dustin, is she ready for your dick?"

"I think she is."

"Then get inside her. Let's give her more pleasure than she has ever known."

Dustin stood up. He put on a condom and slicked up his dick with lube.

She rotated her hips, pushing hard against him, arching to offer Dustin a better vantage to enter her ass. He slid his dick past her ring.

Clint felt her body tense. "Go slow, Dustin."

Dustin moved in and out of Beth. Shortly, she began thrashing over Clint. He pumped her pussy, while Dustin stroked her backside. Over and over. Amazing. Her fingernails clawed at his shoulders. Her head rolled wildly.

"Holy hell." Dustin's eyes widened as his enthusiasm commanded him forward.

Clint watched blissful tears well up in her eyes. He pushed deep, deeper. All three of them moved in concert like finely-tuned instruments.

Clint leaned in and kissed her. She whimpered. The tempo of his strokes increased.

He wanted to feel another joint orgasm. "Dustin, are you close?"

"Yes."

"Beth, are you?"

"Yes, sir."

"Can you let go on my command?"

"Y-Yes, sir."

"I'm ready, too. Both of you, listen to me. Come now."

"G-God." Beth's tears fell to his chest.

"Fuck!" Dustin shouted, evidently shooting his load.

Clint felt his dick pulse from his emptying balls, his whole body participating in the final thrust. His body shuddered. He felt Beth quaking against him. He watched Dustin's face tighten, then slacken.

"That was fucking amazing." Dustin leaned over Beth, kissing her neck, squeezing Clint's hand. "I love you both very much."

"I love you." Beth's eyes locked on Clint's. "I love you both."

All the pain of Clint's life washed away. This was what he had needed for so long. To be loved and to love.

"I love you, Beth. I love you, Dustin. Very much."

* * * *

The last several weeks had been a whirlwind. Quitting the old station hadn't been as tough as Beth thought it would be. Moving in together at the new place, not tough at all, instead it had been wonderful. The new job in New York had been a bit scary, but since she wasn't alone…

"Lady, you need a paddling."

"Dustin, that's about enough of that." Beth sent him a grin.

"Just because you two like to team up against me doesn't mean that I—"

"She said that was enough." Clint winked.

"But Beth never gets enough," Dustin teased.

"You'll never learn, Dustin. If you keep pushing her buttons, you'll lose."

Three months from now, they'd be getting married. One ceremony would include a Justice of the Peace for her and Clint with Dustin as their witness. The other, the *real* one, would be in Maui, just the three of them on the beach at sunset. She'd already written her vows, and she believed Clint had too. Dustin? Well, he'd come up with something amazing on the spot. God, she loved them both so much.

"That's all the time we have for today. This is Comet Radio FM. I'm Dustin."

"I'm Clint."

"And I'm Beth."

In unison, "We're the threesome that heats up New York's mornings."

THE END

www.KrisCook.net

ABOUT THE AUTHOR

A military brat to the core, Kris Cook never put down deep roots in any particular geographic location. Until Texas. Why? Kris loves the sun.

A voracious reader, Kris loves many genres of fiction, but this writer's favorite books are romances that are edgy, sexy, with rich characters and unique challenges. Kris' influences include JR Ward, Lora Leigh, and Shayla Black.

Kris has won and placed in several writing contests in the past couple of years.

Kris' motto: I like cooking up really hot books for my readers. The hotter, the better.

For news, info and upcoming releases, be sure to stop by www.KrisCook.net

Also by Kris Cook

Perfection

Available at
BOOKSTRAND.COM

Siren Publishing, Inc.
www.SirenPublishing.com